Lace For Milady

Joan Smith

ISIS
LARGE PRINT
Oxford

Copyright © Joan Smith, 1980, 2006

First published in Great Britain 2006
by
Robert Hale Limited

Published in Large Print 2007 by ISIS Publishing Ltd.,
7 Centremead, Osney Mead, Oxford OX2 0ES
by arrangement with
Robert Hale Limited

British Library Cataloguing in Publication Data
Smith, Joan, 1938–
    Lace for milady. – Large print ed.
    1. Love stories
    2. Large type books
    I. Title
    813.5'4 [F]

ISBN 978–0–7531–7908–6 (hb)
ISBN 978–0–7531–7909–3 (pb)

Printed and bound in Great Britain by
T. J. International Ltd., Padstow, Cornwall

Lace For Milady

CHAPTER
ONE

They say I am an egotist. I am flattered, though I do not delude myself for a moment that it is intended as a compliment. It is intended as a slur on my particular bent for self-assertion, but it is surely everyone's privilege, if not duty, to tend first to his own garden. In any case, they will find some euphemistic phrase for me now that I am . . . But I get ahead of myself and will begin with my ending if I don't beware. I have never written a story before and am already becoming confused. I shall recommence. My friend tells me it will be a perfect catharsis to purge my soul of all the spleen left behind by recent events. It is more likely to drive me insane, and you, too, if I don't get on with it.

There, he has counted up nine *I*s in the first paragraph and confirmed me as an egotist. So be it. I (again I) am Priscilla Denver. No one has dared to call me Prissie since I was ten, fifteen years ago. If you are any sort of mathematician at all, it is not necessary for me to mention that I am twenty-five years old. I am also unmarried and do not blush to acknowledge the fact. It is no disgrace to have inhabited the planet for a quarter of a century. It is God's will, one assumes. The particular corner of the planet I inhabited for

1

twenty-four of those years was Wiltshire, and it is surely one of the more pleasant corners anywhere, with a pleasing variety of downs, fertile valleys, scattered forests, and streams. I was born in the year of our Lord 1788, but do not fear I mean to bore you with a tedious recital of my childhood. Nothing of the least interest occurred throughout its duration. I was a healthy, normal child, less beautiful than some, and more intelligent than many others. At twenty-one I received an offer of marriage from an eligible gentleman whose name I shall suppress since he is now married to another. He was good enough, but with a tendency to moon about and discuss love as though it were a tangible thing. Also he smoked cigars and did not have his jackets aired afterward, so that the unpleasant odour hung about him. The name — suggests to this day the lingering, sour smell of stale cigar smoke to me. But I digress, friend, and to a subject you dislike, my first lover. Back to the story. I'll never finish it I know. But I shall try to get on with the beginning at least.

My father was a scholar, a purveyor of Greek at Oxford. Mama and I did not accompany him, for females are not welcomed and hardly tolerated in that hallowed atmosphere. We remained at home at Runnymede, named, of course, after that spot where King John was forced to renounce some of his more flagrant abuses by signing the Magna Charta. Our Runnymede was no more than a cosy cottage. Papa always joined us for the summer and added unknowingly to my paltry store of knowledge by leaving his texts lying about. I found some considerable amusement in Electra, Andromeda and other Grecian ladies of antiquity, not the least of which was that grown men, supposedly intelligent ones, wasted their time reading such trash.

But I said I would not bore you with my childhood. There I remained till I was twenty-four. Papa died when I was nineteen, and it made very little difference in our lives except for the summer, when he didn't come home. At twenty-one, my twenty-one, that is, Mama remarried. She chose a well-to-do retired judge from the city, a bachelor. Mama was only forty herself and still handsome. Mr Higgins was considerably older. I did not actively dislike him. Mama died in the second year of that marriage in childbirth. One can only wonder at the ineligibility of a woman her age having a child, but it happened. Mr Higgins was broken-hearted. The child did not survive; it would have been a boy. Nor did the father live much longer. He drank himself to death, quite literally. He was not sober from the day Mama died. I was twenty-four when he died, and I found myself an heiress. Mr Higgins had invested heavily upon 'Change, and I was his sole heir, the possessor of one hundred thousand pounds. I was quite simply delighted. I never thought to be rich but knew there were great advantages pertaining to such a condition.

I have said Papa was a professor of Greek. What I did not mention is that he married above him. Mama was a Devonmoore, claiming kinship to *the* Devonmoores of East Sussex. She was not dramatically cut off by her family, but she dwindled off from them upon her

3

marriage to Papa. She could not continue in her exalted style of living and was too proud to visit her relations in a gig or hired carriage and team, so she did not visit at all. Papa had been hired as a tutor to her cousin, which is how she met him. Though she ceased visiting, she wrote endlessly to her relations for years. After several years, her correspondents had thinned to her older sister Ethelberta.

With a fortune now at my back, I decided to institute a personal relationship with Mama's and my relations. I chose, of course, her most faithful and lasting correspondent, Ethelberta. I wrote first of Mama's death, and again of my step-father's. My aunt replied to both, in the second letter enquiring whether I was "adequately provided for." When she heard by return post just how adequately provided for I was, she immediately asked me to visit her. She had a son in his thirtieth year, unmarried and unhandsome, but I do not say that is why she asked me. Neither do I say it is not.

My Aunt Ethelberta proved to be a snob. I enjoyed her company excessively. I have a suspicion I am a snob myself. She was a snob about genealogy, which she calls quite plainly and somewhat gruesomely blood. If the blue blood has a metallic tinge of gold, it is, of course, all to the good. I am a snob in the matter of intellect; I like my friends to have some accomplishments beyond gossiping and plying their needles. My aunt's accomplishment was riding. She is an excellent horsewoman. She had married "up" as surely as Mama had married "down." My aunt is a lady with a capital *L*. Lady Inglewood, widow of Lord Inglewood, first Baron Inglewood. She would like it immeasurably better if her husband had been sixth or seventh baron, but the fact of the matter is he won a title from that dissipated old dandy, the Prince of Wales, in a game of faro. That is to say, he actually won ten thousand pounds, but with the Prince's chronic state of financial embarrassment, he was willing to settle for paying for a title. I learned all this from her son George, named, of course, after his godfather, that same Prince Regent. My aunt contends the title was given for some vague extraordinary service to the Prince, but the extraordinary service was ten thousand pounds, and I think with a little haggling Lord Inglewood might have been the Earl of Inglewood, but he was not himself socially ambitious, I believe. He should have let his wife do the bargaining for him.

I believe I mentioned my aunt is a widow. What a sad state the medical profession is in that persons in their forties and fifties fall like flies. But then any drinking companion of the Prince Regent is fortunate to reach fifty, which Inglewood did, with a decade to spare. He left his widow a lady, but he also left her with a home mortgaged to the hilt. He was not always so lucky as the night he won his title from Prinny. There was only George to bring the family fortunes about, and it was clearly incumbent upon him to make an advantageous match. Equally clearly, his mama took the ill-conceived idea that I was the well-dowered virgin to be so honoured. I was polite for six days, for I did not wish a rupture with the most elevated member of my family, but when she put the thing into words on the seventh day of my visit, my politeness was at an end.

She said, "You are not young, not pretty, and not well-connected, except for myself, Priscilla. I think it would be greatly to your advantage to marry Lord Inglewood." So fond was she of the title that all references to both her late husband and her living son were couched in terms of Lord Inglewood. It was sometimes confusing, but, of course, on this occasion her meaning was perfectly clear.

"I see no advantage in marrying a penniless cousin I have hardly known a week," I replied quite frankly.

"Penniless! You forget he is Lord Inglewood, Priscilla. Inglewood belongs to him."

"I do not forget it." With great tact I forbore mentioning the impossibility of doing so, with the title constantly ringing in my ears. "But if I am not mistaken, the estate belongs largely to the mortgage lenders."

"You have money, and little enough else, I might tell you. Your father a *teacher*! Really, how Andrea could be so foolish. It is an excellent match in every way, advantages to be gained on both sides. The ages just right, and George is very fond of you."

George, like his papa, is fonder of a wine bottle than the handsomest woman ever born (which I am not); but he did not actively dislike me so far as I could tell. I expect he would do exactly as his mother told him in any case.

There was a little more of the same pointless sort of discussion on the subject, which neither of us allowed to grow into an irreconcilable difference. I, because I wished to keep her friendship, and she, because she wished to have access to my mind to press her point. After a few more bouts, however, the atmosphere about the place became unpleasantly tense. I ceased being Priscilla and became Miss Denver. In the same manner, Aunt Ethelberta became Lady Inglewood, and before any other change of address should occur, I expressed my intention of leaving. Of leaving her roof, that is, but not the neighbourhood.

I had become fascinated by the ocean. It has this effect on some people. I went every afternoon to walk along the shore, and generally saw the same few people there, just gazing at the endless expanse of grey-green water. There was not so much to see: a few fishing boats, more or less whitecaps depending on the weather, and always that smell comprised of salt and water and marine life that is not even very pleasant. I don't know why I was drawn to it. It was the ever-moving, ever-changing pattern of the waves perhaps, or the knowledge that across the Channel lay France, to the west the vast expanse of water with somewhere out there in infinity wild America and cold Canada. It inspired me to think and dream. I hadn't had my fill of it yet, and I would stay in Sussex.

My aunt required money; I required an elegant but not extremely large roof over my head. Being both practical women, a scheme was agreed upon between us. I would rent the Dower House, now standing empty and profitless, for five hundred pounds per annum. It is a very fine home built of grey stone in the Gothic style, with four lancet windows on either side of the handsome oak double doors. It has ornamental flying buttresses, finials, gargoyles, and all the customary trappings of a Gothic building. I confess I liked very well the notion of living in an old mansion. In my youth I had been addicted to Gothic novels — I mean my extreme youth, fourteen or fifteen. By sixteen I had outgrown such mawkish stuff; but every stage we go through leaves its mark on us, and the mark that Mrs Radcliffe left on me was a quite irrational desire to live in an old Gothic mansion. Now that I had independence, I would do so.

The next half of this chapter may give you the idea I am a fool. I am not, but I behaved foolishly, I admit, with regard to the Dower House. I fell in love with it. My emotions, unmoved throughout the years by mere human flesh, succumbed to a passion for wood and stones and mortar. It was not in the best repair. I wished to get at it with my imagination and money and return it to its former glory, but I retained enough sanity not to do this to someone else's house. I wanted it for my own, and offered to buy it. It belonged to my aunt outright. It was not part of the estate of Inglewood, which surprised and delighted me. She accepted my offer, which also surprised and delighted me. Of course she did not accept it quickly; she screwed me up to a very good price. My Aunt Ethelberta, who had become my aunt again and not Lady Inglewood once I left her home, behaved criminally, in my opinion, but was crafty enough to do

8

it legally. If that is a contradiction — well, of course, it is technically, so I shall say instead she behaved reprehensibly. She defrauded her own niece. She purposely misrepresented the Dower House to me as an ancient home. I subsequently learned it was less than one hundred years old. Very likely I could have sued her for fraudulent misrepresentation or some such thing, but she was my aunt, and I did not wish a scandal in the neighbourhood. She also misrepresented other things, *grossly* misrepresented them. I would have hired a solicitor had I suspected treachery and double-dealing from my own kin. I do not disdain to seek professional help in the least, despite the opinion of certain people who will read this with a hateful smirk and think "it served you right."

I have already said the house was practically new, and no doubt you are raising your brows and thinking I was easily cozzened after calling myself intelligent. I think in the same case you would have been, too. It was newly built, but of old stones, and in the style of an older period, built as a sort of miniature Belview, in fact, an old and famous home nearby of which I shall speak again soon (and often). I only discovered the house's true age when I pulled back a rambling vine from the keystone over the door and saw to my horror the numbers 1733. The other deception in the case was the truly serious one, however, but I didn't discover it for another two weeks. With an effort, I shall keep it for its rightful place in this tale, though my pen itches to jot it down now.

She sold me the place furnished and fully equipped. Naturally I was familiar with the state and quality of the furnishings by this time. I was not fooled into thinking that extremely ugly old tables of plain deal were the work of Kent or anything of the sort. The stuff was old and serviceable, not beautiful. Draperies and carpets would all have to go, in degrees, but I looked forward to these changes. I could afford them and meant to do the place up in fine style. I did not go to the cellars, and accepted her word that there were good wine cellars, but in fact there were exactly twelve bottles of wine there when I finally got around to examining it. She had not actually said there was anything in the cellars, though the term "a good wine cellar" does not generally refer to architecture. My grounds kept shrinking by the day, till in the end I barely had an acre of garden fore and aft to call my own. As you may imagine, battles on all these points were waged, but between battles Lady Inglewood (and sometimes Aunt Ethelberta) helped us in various ways, so that a sort of superficial peace reigned between us. We visited back and forth, and in her mind the wish was still alive that George might marry my fortune. He continued to call regularly. Even when his mother and I were completely at odds, George came.

Slack, my companion, has just read my account thus far, and though she did not say so, I see she is miffed that she has not entered the pages. It is an unaccountable oversight on my part. Naturally I did not set up house without a suitable companion to lend me countenance. Indeed, she is more than a companion. She has been my faithful friend forever; all through my childhood in Wiltshire she was my nanny, governess, abigail. She was some connection of Papa's and came to his home when I was born to lend a hand. She never left it, and I trust she will never leave me. Now, in case her head expands unduly at this description, let me go on to give her a character sketch. She is honest, bossy, over-bearing, short-tempered and clever. Slack is twice my own age. She has black hair and one black eyebrow that runs across her forehead like a narrow velvet ribbon. Her eyes are grey and as sharp as a lynx's, her nose is sharp, as is her tongue.

There — she has been back and read it, and is more miffed than ever. She suggests I draw a pen sketch of myself, and points out that what I said of her goes well beyond a character study. I thought I had explained my appearance, but she says not, I only stated I was not a pretty child. I am also not a pretty woman. I am five feet six inches tall, have an athletic build, brown hair and brown eyes. My teeth are in good repair. I am fastidious about my teeth, not primarily for purposes of vanity, but because I had an abscessed tooth drawn when I was eight, and it is not a procedure I wish to have repeated on my adult teeth.

We went on together with our little domestic ups and downs at the Dower House, Slack and I. I began fixing the place up, beginning with the main saloon, where I installed rose velvet draperies. While in the drapery shop in Pevensey, I also purchased material for two new gowns, to suit my new status as a home-owner and occasional hostess. Having been in mourning and half-mourning for over five years all told, with the deaths of Papa, Mama, and Mr Higgins, I was naturally eager to get out of it. It was six months since the demise of Mr Higgins. I bore him considerable gratitude for leaving me his fortune but had small traces of love or even respect for a man foolish enough to drink himself into his grave over the death of a wife of only two years' duration. At six months I was in half-mourning, with the intention lurking at the back of my mind to put off all remnants of crape entirely.

"Rag-mannered," Slack told me bluntly when I got home with my gold-striped lutestring and my green Italian silk.

"You might have mentioned it in the shop," I replied in the same tone.

"And announced to the town your step-father is still warm in his grave? I wished to save at least a semblance of decency, since it seems we are to *live* here." Slack was not yet completely resigned to our permanent remove to Sussex.

"Very clever. I doubt anyone here knows a thing about me but that I am an heiress. Lady Inglewood would not have told anyone I am in mourning for it was, and is, her intention to see me a bride within a month. I am mighty tired of decking myself out like a carrion crow, Slack, and mean to get into some colours before I am too old."

Any reference to age is greeted with a sniff by Slack. She had passed the half century on her last birthday. Streaks of grey begin to lighten her black hair, but I hold the unspoken suspicion that as with many spinsters, a ray of hope shines yet that she will meet and marry some dashing Prince Charming. It is foolish in the extreme, of course. At twenty-two I put aside all such thoughts and would have set on my caps except that they are a nuisance. Women are already so encumbered with camisoles and petticoats that any additional item of clothing is to be eschewed.

I paid no heed to Slack's repeated remonstrances regarding the yellow lutestring and green silk but purchased the latest copy of *La Belle Assemblée* in town and selected two suitable patterns. Suitable to me, that is; Slack did not approve. She suggested that as it was obviously my intention to set up as the village flirt, I ought to hire a fashionable modiste to cut my gowns for me, and added sundry ill-natured hints regarding decolletage and making sure the skirt hugged the hips tightly, and suggested vulgar coquelicot ribbons for the green silk. So suitable for *Christmas*, she said.

"I hope you pass swiftly through the delicate age you are at, Slack," I told her, "for I find your conversation recently disagreeable in the extreme."

The yellow lutestring was cut high at the neck, as became one of my years, with a long sleeve and a full skirt that allowed a good walking pace. The green silk would have been similarly styled had Slack not enraged me with her ceaseless jibes. In retaliation, I had it cut low enough to expose more of my chest than had been formerly shown to the world, and did take in the waist and hips sufficiently to give an indication of my figure. In fact, when I stood before my mirror, I doubted I would have the nerve to appear in public in the outfit, and cursed Slack's humour and my temper that had caused me to ruin a guinea's worth of good material. It was quite dashing, but it was not *me*.

Lady Inglewood raised her brows when I first called in the yellow striped, but as it caused George to evince more interest than formerly in me, she did not object verbally.

I enjoyed those first few weeks at the Dower House. There was sufficient novelty in coming to a new place and making new friends, trimming up my home to a more stylish appearance and generally getting the lie of the land to keep me entertained. I had my walks along the beach that still amused me, and I had my carriage to drive me to town. I felt life could offer little more. But as August drew to a close and September came upon us, I began to perceive that the keening winds of winter would make my walks along the sea uncomfortable. It was then I took the decision to buy myself a mount. I had procured before coming to Sussex the team to pull my carriage, and had a small stable set up, so why not add a hack to it? I had always wanted to ride. My first attempt along this line led to a new acquaintance and several other items of interest, so I shall make it a new chapter.

Slack is sitting across the room rattling the newspaper impatiently, which means she wants her tea and my company. Truth to tell, I find this writing business tedious enough that I could do with a cup of tea myself. I shall resume the chronicle tomorrow.

CHAPTER
TWO

When I read a book, I like to have an idea how my characters look. Not that I adhere slavishly to the author's description — I usually give the hero black hair, whatever his creator decrees, and the heroine blonde, but still one likes to have some general notion, and as I have mentioned Lady Ing, as Slack and I took to calling my aunt, several times, I shall essay my hand at a portrait. She is short but appears tall. I don't know how she achieves it, a throwing back of her shoulders and tilting her chin up perhaps cause the eyes to travel upward. She has a truly hideous, brindled shade of hair, brownish-red turning to grey, that she wears in a complicated arrangement of loops and swirls. With this awful mop she chooses purple and bile green gowns — one colour at a time, that is, not a mixture. She has close-set dark eyes and a sharp nose not unlike Slack's. Her voice is both nasal and strident, the unloveliest part of the woman. She walks with short, quick steps, jerky, unbecoming, and is not at all like my mama. All this unattractive appearance is forgotten when she gets atop her mount. As I have mentioned, she is an accomplished horsewoman, an accomplishment I admire but do not envy, as certain people have hinted.

Having few close friends as yet, I approached my aunt on the subject of buying a mount. I felt the duty would devolve on George, and was willing to accept this.

She surprised me, as she usually managed to do. "I'll sell you Juliette," she said at once. Juliette was her own mount, a highbred mare, really very handsome, indeed, a bay. I had often seen the two of them going across the park or down the road, and when I thought of riding, I thought of myself riding something akin to Juliette.

"What will you ride yourself?" I asked her.

"I am reaching the age where I must give it up. I have a little twinge of pain in my elbows that is worse after riding." She looked still young enough and spry enough to ride for ten years, but I did not question her. I presume she knew if her elbows ached.

"Very well. What price do you want for her?"

"One hundred and fifty pounds."

The speed of her answer caused me to wonder whether she hadn't been considering this sale for some time. No need to include the negotiations that lowered the price to one hundred. I had decided that was my top price, and once she realized this the thing was as well as done. She got the better part of the fifty pounds out of me by adding an extra charge for saddle, blankets, curry brushes, and other objects, and I believe we were both satisfied with our bargain. As Juliette was no gift horse, I did not hesitate to look her thoroughly in the mouth, legs, chest, and eyes. I did not intend to repeat the dowsing I had taken on my house. I now required a riding habit but could not wait to try my skill, and went to the stable straight away to do so. With the help of a groom, a block of wood, and strong arms, I contrived to get myself hoisted aloft.

I am not chicken-hearted. No foolish fears of mice, heights, the dark or small spaces trouble me, but I confess that when first I looked down to the ground, I felt a quiver of apprehension. I grabbed the reins awkwardly, and they seemed but a poor means of holding myself on to the animal's back. To ensure my seat, I put one hand in Juliette's mane. She did not appear to object to this. In fact, I later was told that horses have little feeling in this area, and it is recommended to do this when learning to jump. This felt a little safer, and I let Juliette out of the stable. The ground ceased whirling under me after two slow walks around the garden, and I was emboldened to let her out a little. The groom informed me to give her a little kick with my heel to achieve this. I did so, and she walked faster but not dangerously fast. I have said my land was only two acres, but mean as she was, Lady Ing did not prohibit my walking in her park, and I assumed riding, too, would be permitted. The lands between our two houses were open, a meadow and a garden, whereas I required, or at least desired, the concealing privacy of a few trees for my first ride, so I went off into the spinney that did not belong to her. It belonged to the Duke of Clavering, my neighbour on the other side, and was a part of Belview, his estate. He had a reputation for liking his privacy very well, but as he was known to be in London, I had no fear of discovery.

The ride proceeded satisfactorily. I had no illusion my performance rivalled that of Juliette's former owner, but I did not fall off, and eventually even let go of her mane and held myself on by the reins alone. I am fairly athletic. I came to enjoy sitting so high in the saddle and was eager to try something more daring than a walk. I kicked Juliette's side, a little harder than I had intended to, actually, and she broke into a trot. It was somewhat frightening. The smoothness of the walk was all disrupted, and I found myself bumping up and down. I grabbed her mane again, and as I lurched forward to do so, my heel inadvertently touched Juliette's side once more. The silly animal — really, horses are the most stupid creatures, ten times dumber than a pig — thought I wished to go faster, and did so. I was positively flopping in the saddle now, and becoming quite frightened. Worse was soon to come. The saddle began slipping on me, slipping so that I was virtually hanging off Juliette's left side. This unnerved the animal, and she took to going faster and faster. I soon realized my best option was to fall off before I got trampled under her hooves, and let go, rolling in the damp earth of the spinney. I did not break any bones, fortunately, but I wrenched my left knee rather badly. It was my pride that was the more hurt, and I was thankful I had taken my first lesson and inevitable tumble in the privacy of the spinney.

It soon dawned on me that my disgrace would not be kept to myself. Juliette, the perverse animal, did not stop. She kept on going, and I had a sinking sensation that where she would go eventually was back to her stall at Inglewood. I could hear her go forward, galloping now. I was very relieved I had had the presence of mind

18

to get off before she took into that wicked gallop. The hooves were thundering in the distance, then a shout rang out.

"Ho, Julie — Whoa, Julie" — something of the sort. It was a man's voice. It seemed the Duke of Clavering's game warden was in the spinney, and I was glad he would retrieve the animal for me before it bolted back to its former owner. The hooves fell silent and some indistinct words were said to Juliette, who whinnied playfully in reply. "Here! Bring her here!" I shouted, and tried to arise. My knee gave a sharp stab of pain, and I sank to the ground again. I was embarrassed to be found crouching there, but the man was only a game warden after all. In roughly two minutes he had followed the path and found me. He looked no better than a game warden should look. A large, brawny man outfitted in an indifferent blue jacket and buckskins. His hair was black and his face swarthy, the result of his outdoors occupation, I assumed. The eyes, too, were dark. The man might have been a gypsy.

"Took a tumble, did you?" he asked, with a somewhat superior smile on his face. He did not dismount, having no manners, but remained in his saddle, holding Juliette's reins.

"Certainly not. I merely decided to dismount, for Juliette was going faster than I liked."

"Dismount? Ah, is that what the ladies call falling off a horse nowadays? Next time you wish to slacken the pace. I suggest you pull on the reins, slowly and evenly." He smiled on me condescendingly from atop his horse.

"Next time you discover a lady stretched out on the ground, I suggest you dismount and help her up instead of delivering a quite unnecessary lecture," I replied tartly, and picked myself up with no help from the man. I took a pace toward Juliette; my knee buckled under me, and I half fell.

That, finally, was sufficient to get him down from his animal. It was also sufficient to widen the grin on his face. "I'll toss you up," he offered, and went on to do precisely that.

Before I knew what he was about, he had placed his two hands around my waist and lifted me from the ground as though I were an elf, and I weigh nearly nine stone. By making a wild lunge at mane and reins, I managed somehow to get on Juliette's back. The trouble, or part of it, was immediately made clear. The saddle was buckled on so loosely that the lurching movement drew it around one hundred and eighty degrees when I pulled on the pommel, and I was once again on the ground, holding in my temper at this stupid man.

"Thank you very much indeed!" I said, and arose, though my knee still ached.

"I take it this is your maiden ride?" he enquired, grinning wider and wider till I feared his face would split.

"As you so cleverly deduce, it is my maiden ride."

"Lesson number one: Always check that the girth is buckled on tightly. And while we are about it, lesson number two: Don't clutch at the reins as though they were the handle of your reticule. They are held thus."

He reached to his own reins and wound them through his fingers in a quite complicated and uncomfortable-looking manner. "Their purpose is *not* to hold you on, but merely to direct the animal."

I feigned deafness, grabbing the reins. "I'll bear it in mind," I said, then began walking home. Not for fifty pounds would I have got on that animal's back again in front of anyone.

"If you don't do it now, you never will," he said, apparently reading my mind. "Here, let me tighten her girth for you. You can't walk back all the way with that game leg."

"I am not a horse, sir. I do not have a *game leg*, or a swollen fetlock. I have wrenched my knee, and I shall walk home."

"Suit yourself," he answered with the utmost indifference, then putting one toe in the stirrup, he threw the other leg over the horse's back with the greatest of ease, and it was a huge beast, and a stallion at that, which seemed very vicious looking to me. He commenced walking along after me. I turned and tried to be rid of him.

"I don't require an escort, thank you."

"You will require further assistance before you've gone much further."

"I haven't far to go."

"You have over a mile."

I couldn't believe it was so far till I had been walking — limping, really — ten minutes and still saw no end to the spinney. The man then got down and suggested rather forcefully that I try riding again. He tightened the beast's saddle, and once again tossed me up. "I'll hold her reins and walk if you're afraid," he offered.

This offer was spurned, but I took care to keep Juliette's pace to a strict walk, which was very uncomfortable because it meant holding my feet well out from her sides. Before we had gone much farther, the back of the Dower House was visible over the thinning trees. I was never so glad to see a pile of rocks in my life.

"I'll see you in," the man said when we got to the stable.

"That is really not at all necessary."

"I want to talk to you," he said, in an authoritative voice that I suddenly realized spoke in cultured accents. I had been too upset before to remark it.

"Who are you?" I asked, rather bluntly, I'm afraid.

"Clavering. Your neighbour on the east."

"The Duke of Clavering?" I asked, quite simply astonished. No elegance, no manners — a gypsy.

"At your service, whenever you care to take a tumble, ma'am," he answered, and offered me his arm.

"I thought you were in London."

"I was. I returned. Shall we go?"

I couldn't think of a sensible word to say, so said nothing. Immediately we were in, I went to my room to clean up, asking Slack to get His Grace a glass of wine. When I returned downstairs fifteen minutes later, he sat making himself quite at home with Slack. She, however, is never completely at home with any male over eight or ten, and was looking grim.

22

"What was it you wished to speak to me about?" I asked a little sharply. In the normal way I would have been friendlier with a neighbour, but having shown myself in so poor a light, I was angry.

"About Seaview," he replied, equally bluntly.

"And what might Seaview be?" I asked.

"It's here. The Dower House," Slack informed me.

"Oh, you mean it already has a name. I had rather looked forward to naming it myself. I had thought of Hillcrest, for we are at the crest of the hill, you know."

"Your neighbour a mile down the road had the same original notion. McCurdys call their place Hillcrest. The hill actually crests there. You have a view of the sea; we called it Seaview."

"We?" I asked, with perhaps a touch of condescension, or so Slack told me later. Actually "as jealous as a cat of her new-born litter" is the simile she used.

"It was named by my great-grandfather, since he built it," Clavering informed me, in much the same possessive tone.

Lady Ing ought to have told me this. The impression given by her was that it was a part of the original Inglewood holding. I had wondered at the time that it was in her power to sell it, and not a word had she said of all this. Of course she had also implied it was three or four hundred years old, and that had proven untrue. So it was some Clavering, unless the man facing me lied, who had inscribed the telltale date on that key-stone.

"I see. I hadn't realized that," I answered, pretending no more than a decent modicum of interest.

"Did Lady Inglewood not tell you so when she sold you the place?"

"No, she did not consider it of sufficient importance apparently."

"But she told you about the leased land?"

This was the manner in which I made the horrendous discovery about my precious Gothic mansion. I have given a hint of double-dealing and treachery on my aunt's part. This is it. My pen shakes in anger yet to write it. "What leased land?" I asked. Something in his triumphant, gloating expression made me expect trouble ahead.

"The land on which Seaview stands," he answered, relishing his victory.

"No, no, I bought the land outright from her. It is a very small area, of course, only a couple of acres, but it is not leased."

"It was not hers to sell."

I was on my feet, and soon falling awkwardly to my chair again, for the twisted knee really hurt quite abominably. "What do you mean? What are you telling me?" I demanded, incredulous.

"What I can scarcely believe you do not know already. Seaview stands on land leased from me."

"But — but I don't understand. How can this be? She couldn't sell me a house without land for it to stand on. It is ridiculous. I never heard of such a thing in my life. Slack, get the papers, the ownership papers."

Slack was nearly as upset as I was myself, and bustled from the room in a swirl of black skirts. Slack never wore a thing but black.

While awaiting her return, I asked the Duke, "Just how did such a state of affairs come about? How did the Inglewoods come to build on your ..." Then I stopped. "But you said your ancestors built the place. How does it come to be out of your hands?"

He looked inordinately pleased at the tizzy into which he had thrown me, and I resolved to show less of my concern. He answered blandly, "My great-grandfather built the place for his sister-in-law, who was a Tilbridge. She was an invalid and required a place by the sea, right on the sea. The solarium was built for her convenience."

I believe I have neglected to mention elsewhere in this disjointed story that Seaview has a solarium, which is nothing other than a large, glassed-in porch that is too hot in summer and I am convinced will be uncomfortably draughty in winter. A useless thing, and not very attractive either since it ruins the lines of the place, sticking out between two sham flying buttresses as it does. Slack has put forward the idea of using it for a conservatory, but at the moment it holds no more than three geraniums, rapidly turning yellow since we don't often remember to water them.

He continued, "Miss Tilbridge left the place to a niece, and after a few more changes of hands in various wills it fell into Lady Inglewood's family. Our two families are connected slightly through marriage. But it is not the custom ever for any of my family to let land go irrecoverably out of our hands, and at the end of ninety-nine years the land is to revert to Claverings, whatever about the house."

"How many years of the lease are up?" I asked. I thought from his wiley smile he was about to say ninety-eight, but it wasn't quite that desperate.

"Eighty," he said.

It was a frightful blow. That my aunt would play such a low, underhanded trick was bad enough, that I who prided myself a little on my intelligence should be such an easy dupe was worse, but the most severe blow, of course, was that I didn't own the land on which my house stood.

Before I was required to reply, Slack was back, puffing from a very fast dash to the strongbox where vital documents are kept. She waved them in her hands, pulling off the ribbons and opening them to read in detail what we should have read before. She read aloud the legal mumbojumbo of parties of the first part and parties of the second part, and with an impatient hand I grabbed them from her, to find myself, too, in a sea of heretofores and aforementioneds.

"If you will permit me," Clavering said, and held out a peremptory hand for the papers. He turned them over to the last page, and there in fine print, though no finer than the rest of the document, to be fair, were the accursed words. "The property held in lease by the Duke of Clavering till January 1, A.D. 1832, at which time it reverts to his sole ownership and discretion."

He held the page in one hand and pointed out the relevant passage with a surprisingly well-shaped finger of the other. On his small finger of the pointing hand a heavy gold ring sat, catching the glow from the sun in a large emerald. Still when I think of my poor leased land, I think of that pointing finger, like a finger of fate, and the green stone winking somberly in the sun. I read it once, twice, a third time. The words did not change, and I could still not believe it.

"Do you mean to say that, that — *woman* sold me a house that has no land to go with it?" I stormed futilely.

"It certainly seems you made the error of buying a house that stands on land belonging to me," he agreed with a truly hateful look. Not a smirk but a suppressed smirk, which is infinitely worse. "Tell me, was the purchase, like your ride, a first?"

"Yes, and like the ride, I took a fall, but this is not the end of it."

He lifted the documents from my fingers. I had snatched them back from him, but he now scanned the papers casually. "Everything here is in order. What do you hope to do about it?"

"Wring her neck," I said grimly.

"That will help cool your anger, but little else. I have a more practical suggestion to rectify your error."

I looked my question, too distraught to speak, but quite aware of that unnecessary "your error."

"Sell Seaview to me," he said.

"No!" The response was instinctive. It came out without thought or effort on my part, but it was my feeling. I loved my old sham Gothic mansion. It was like a little fairy castle, a miniature castle on miniature grounds, but it was what I wanted. Inside it was well divided with a few large rooms. I liked the view of the sea, and in spite of her criminal tendencies, I liked dealing with Aunt Ethelberta, too. I had no desire to leave Sussex.

"I know you paid too much for the place, but I am willing to purchase it from you at the same price," he said reasonably.

I suspected the price I had paid Lady Ing was a good one, though the estate agent in Pevensey assured me it was not exorbitant. Her good friend, no doubt.

"How do you know what I paid for it?" I asked. It seemed the Duke knew a great deal more about me than I knew about him. He knew where I lived when we had met in the spinney, and though I couldn't remember having a name put to me, no doubt he knew that as well.

"I took the trouble to find out. Three thousand pounds, was it not?"

"Yes, it was, and I do not consider it excessive."

"Considering the unusual circumstance of the leased land, I doubt she would have found many takers, but, of course, you know what it is worth to you to live for nineteen years in a draughty, uncomfortable, decrepit old house."

Every instinct demanded a rude reply to this speech, but it was my desire to ingratiate the Duke to get him to renew the lease for another ninety-nine years, so I held in my anger. "Surely another lease can be arranged . . ." I began placatingly.

"I think not."

"You have no need of it! Belview is *huge*." Clavering's home was a spot known to me only by reputation. So far as actual appearance went, I had seen

28

no more than a tantalizing hint or two from behind the treed park. A branch of beech would sway to reveal a crenellated edge of roof standing against the sky, or a glimpse of a turret, or bartizan swelling out from a corner.

"I do not require it for myself, but I require it."

"What for?"

The black brows rose perceptibly, and a spark of anger lit his dark eyes. He suddenly looked more duke than gypsy. His Grace was not accustomed to account to anyone for his whims. He hesitated long enough for me to realize the question was an impertinence. At length he replied unhelpfully, "For a relative."

"It is said that Belview has fifty bedrooms. I can't think one of them could not house your relative."

Again there was a pause, then he decided to humour me with an answer. "Sixty actually, but my aunt is ill — lung trouble — and requires sea air without the inconvenience of a large house. Seaview is closer to the sea than I am, and it has the solarium."

One would think his aunt was to have the "inconvenience" of polishing the floors and windows to hear him speak. "It isn't that much closer, and as to the solarium it is more of a nuisance than anything else. It is very uncomfortable. We never use it."

"You are not invalids. My aunt would use it."

"She will not use it for nineteen years, sir. By that time I trust she will be either recovered to health or dead."

"Suit yourself. You have made a bad bargain, and I thought any *intelligent* person would be happy to extricate herself so easily. You will find no surfeit of buyers for a house that boasts no land of its own, not even the ground it stands on."

"I don't want a surfeit of buyers, or even one."

Again that maddening, superior smile was on his hateful gypsy face. "You will look nohow when it is discovered in Pevensey how Lady Inglewood gulled you," he said, trying a new tack to make me sell.

"I don't care what anyone thinks of me."

"I thought otherwise. Your quite foolish, and really very dangerous maiden ride in a spinney without a groom to help you led me to believe you preferred to keep your blunders to yourself. You should take your first lessons in a clear area that offers soft falling and no dangerous trees or obstacles. An enclosed field is recommended. And *never* alone, just in case you should get thrown — or dismount precipitately — and hurt your knee."

"I did not dismount precipitately."

"You did not dismount at all, madam. The word denotes some choice in the matter. You fell, due to your unique method of buckling the girth loosely. If you ever screw up your courage to try it again, get some help. And you would do better to get yourself a tame mount rather than tackling that spitfire Lady Inglewood keeps. I'm surprised she would let you out on such a spirited mount."

"She has nothing to say about what I ride. She is not my chaperon."

"Surely she has something to say about your ruining her favourite mount's mouth with that manner in which you clutch at the reins."

"Juliette is my horse."

"Good God! Gulled again," he said, in a choking voice, and went off into a series of ill-bred chuckles. He arose, still laughing. "I come to see you will be extremely easy to deal with. You will *buy* anything, and I have some hope that you will also *sell* me Seaview before many days are out."

"*Hillcrest* is not far sale."

"I am not interested in buying McCurdy's place. It is this house that stands on my land I am after. And shall get, *tard ou tôt*. Good day, ma'am." He executed two abbreviated bows toward Slack and myself and left.

"I never met such an insufferably rude man in my life," I said to Slack.

"Sell it," she replied.

"Sell Hillcrest! I wouldn't sell it for the world."

"You never called it Hillcrest before today, and it is too foolish to start doing so now, only because the Duke says it is called Seaview. He is a nasty, foreign-looking person to be sure, and not to be trusted any more than any other man, but still he offered a fair bargain, and I'm surprised you didn't leap at it."

"Why does he want it? Why should he want this little place when he owns Belview, a monstrous house, and half the land between here and Dover. No, Slack, there is something afoot here, and I mean to find out what it is."

My next move was to go storming over to Lady Inglewood's and give her the sharp edge of my tongue. She was very civil, as she always is when she has won a point and knows very well she has been dishonest.

"Oh, my dear, you are limping. I hope you didn't take a spill from Juliette."

She wore bile green today, draped to reveal the layer of fat that encircled her waist like a cincture.

"No, I twisted my knee coming down the stairs. The corner of the carpet at the bottom of the stairs is loose, but I shall have it repaired." Slack scowled at me, for she is a demon for honesty. "I like Juliette very much. I have had my first ride, and we go on famously."

She looked unconvinced, and so, of course, knew very well she had sold me a mount much too frisky for my nonexistent skills, but it was the leased land I had come to argue about and was not to be diverted by a trifle. "I have sustained a call from the Duke of Clavering," I said, squaring my shoulders for battle.

"So unpleasant for you," was her commiserating reply.

"Unpleasant in the extreme, to discover my land is not my own."

"Oh, you refer to the leased land. But of course that is all in the papers. You knew that. I made no effort to conceal it. No one would sign such an important document without reading it all."

"You never mentioned a word of it!"

"You never asked."

"I never asked if the house were yours to sell either. I assumed that when my *own aunt* . . ."

"We discussed, I believe, the matter of the Dower House not being entailed with the estate but my own personal property."

32

This was her line, and she stuck to it buckle and thong. She let fall a few casual mentions of having consulted her solicitor on the matter, which I make no doubt she had done. "So it is all legal, and you must speak to Clavering on the matter. He will renew the lease, for a price."

"I have spoken to him. He won't renew it."

"Pshaw! Of course he will. What did you offer him?"

"I didn't offer him anything."

"Well, my dear, you can't expect something for nothing. Make him an offer. Say five hundred pounds for another ninety-nine years. See if he don't jump at it."

"No, he wants to buy the place from me."

"Does he indeed?" she asked, with a light of interest in her eyes. "Did he mention a price . . .?"

"Yes, he offered me the price I paid for it, though of course, he found it *very high*, considering the leased land," I added with a glare.

"Well, there you are, then. If you dislike the bargain we made, you can be out of it easily enough and no harm done."

This was so patently true that I found myself at *point non plus*. I could hardly complain about the deal when it could be undone with a word.

We — for, of course, Slack accompanied me on this important visit — were left without a thing to say, and settled in for a chat. We had a cup of bohea and some of my aunt's really lovely scones. She relented and gave Slack the recipe for them on that day — a treat formerly denied us. We were returned to superficial terms of amity. It was usually thus between us. We were at undeclared war but claiming friendship because of kinship. I imagine it is the manner in which many families go on. But enough philosophizing. The door knocker sounds, and I must hide these pages in a drawer or find someone perusing them whom I would prefer not to do so till I have glanced over them and seen if I have been too harsh on anyone.

CHAPTER
THREE

The fact of George's being absent when we called upon my aunt that afternoon necessitated his coming that evening to woo me. George, I presumed, took after his papa. He bore no resemblance to his mother. He was a tall, gangly, unprepossessing gentleman, with lank brown hair, a weak chin, and a mouth that had two positions, sulking and grinning. It is difficult to determine which was the less appealing. He wore mouth number two when he entered, grinning. I suppose the grin is actually the less repulsive of the two. Grown men ought not to sulk.

"I hear Clavering was to call," he said, before ever he took a seat.

"Yes, he called early this afternoon."

"Odd he is at home. With autumn coming on he is usually in London. He is active in Parliament, you know."

"I didn't know," I replied, with no effort to feign interest.

"Oh, yes, very active, though I don't know exactly what it is he does. He is a Whig. But there has been a spot of trouble lately with the Gentlemen, and he might be here to look into that."

"What gentlemen?" I asked, with some curiosity.

"The Gentlemen," he repeated. George is not bright. Sometimes it is necessary to rephrase a question three or four times before he understands it. Even this does not ensure a meaningful reply. On this occasion, Slack devised the second rendition.

"This is Whig gentlemen you're talking about, is it, George?" Slack is altogether incomprehensible to me. She dislikes ninety-nine men out of a hundred, but for some obscure reason, she has taken a liking to George and treats him with not only civility but downright kindness.

"Lord, no. I mean the smugglers," he replied, giving us at last his meaning.

"Smugglers?" Slack gasped. I did not gasp. I had heard mention in town of smuggling activities going forth. It is only to be expected on the coast, of course.

"What sort of trouble has there been?" I enquired.

"Caught a bunch of them red-handed. Clavering takes a dim view of smuggling. He'll speak to the magistrate and see they're dealt with severely."

"What has Clavering to say about it?"

"He pretty well runs things hereabouts. Well, a Duke, and his family have been forever. There is no point Mama telling me *I* ought to . . ." Perhaps he forgot his mother's instructions to him. "He has the magistrates and all the politicians in his pocket."

"I am surprised he wastes his time with such a petty matter," I said. "Surely with the war on and the country in such an abominable state, with everyone being taxed to death and the drop in value of the pound eating up the little that is left us, a politician should be better occupied than out chasing a few miserable smugglers."

"Well, he is a law and order man," George explained. "Then, too, there were hunters caught on his lands lately, and that would annoy him no end."

"Any gentleman who owns the better part of a county must expect that," I replied irately.

"Not Clavering. He's posted, and they oughtn't to have been on his land."

"What do you mean, posted?"

"Why, he's put his signs up. You must have seen his signs. Hunting is not allowed on private property if the owner posts signs. Otherwise, of course, those entitled to hunt may hunt anywhere. Game laws," George explained, rather inadequately.

"Do you mean to tell me, George, that any man with a gun may go on any other man's property and shoot his game?"

"Certainly not! Only owners of land worth more than a hundred pounds a year, the eldest sons of squires or higher-placed persons, or lessees of land worth one hundred and fifty a year are allowed to hunt game."

"But they may do so *anywhere*? They could go on your land or mine and shoot our rabbits and we couldn't stop them?"

"Certainly you can run them off, but they are allowed to come on unless told otherwise."

"I never heard of such a thing in my life!" I declared. I first doubted George had the thing straight, but if there was one thing he did know, it was hunting, and the wealth of detail he was in possession of denoted real knowledge. He would not have the wits to make up arbitrary figures.

"The act was passed in 1671 and is still in effect," he informed, finding no fault with this iniquitous situation. "If you don't want them on your land, of course, you can kill your own foxes, for it's mostly fox they shoot. But then if you kill your foxes, the rabbits breed like rabbits." He detected no humour in this comparison. "Really it's six of one and half a dozen of t'other. Clavering killed his foxes, dashed bounder, but his lands are alive with rabbits and badgers and all the smaller game that don't get ate up by the foxes. Dandy shooting at Belview there'd be if it weren't for the traps."

"What sort of traps has he set?" I asked.

"Mantraps. He has the place littered with them. But he's posted, and there's nothing can be done. Clavering, after all." It was sufficient. The Duke of Clavering could lay out mantraps to maim and kill innocent passersby, and so long as he posted it, nothing could be done. Any illiterate who did not understand the signs and decided to take a shortcut through one of his fields might lose a leg, or his life. That would make no difference to him. This ruthlessness tallied very well with the opinion I held of the man, but why should anyone be so selfish?

"Why does he do it?" I asked George.

He shrugged his sloping shoulders. "Says it's to protect his ruins." This was typical George-talk. Uninformative.

"What ruins is this you're talking about?" Slack asked, knowingI would phrase the question less politely.

"Some old falling-apart bit of a church or some such thing on his lands, in the meadow, I believe. It's supposed to be built on top of a Roman temple, and he wants to protect it. He collects rubbish found about his place — Roman rubbish."

"*Roman* rubbish? How would he find such ancient things?" I asked.

"This place is full of old Roman ruins. There must have been hundreds of Romans living here at one time. Clavering has a whole room full of broken jugs and whatnot. Likes them better than real ones. He can tell you to a year or two how old they are. The older they are, the better he likes them."

"He didn't look like a scholar to me," I said.

"Scholar? No such a thing. Just collects things, that's all. Collects other things, too. Has a Marine Room he calls it, with glass cabinets full of shells."

"And is now taking up house collecting," I said stiffly. "The acquisitive instinct is strong in him."

Before George made any reply, there was a diversion in the room. The grate, and indeed the mantelpiece over it, gave a great jump, as though the whole thing were about to fall through the floor.

"What on earth was that?" Slack shouted.

"Grate bumping," George replied, uninformative as ever. We had noticed the grate was bumping.

"What could have caused it?" Slack asked him, since he did not appear to view this bizarre occurrence as unusual at all.

"Happens off and on," he told us. "Took to bumping a few years ago and gives a good rattle every now and again. The house settling it could be."

"A house going on a hundred years old must be settled already. It wasn't that," I informed him.

"Well, it happens anyway. Nothing to worry about. It's why the Seymours left. Or part of the reason. Mama had rented it to them a year or so ago, but the bumping grate worried them. And the other noises. Daresay you don't believe in ghosts, Priscilla?"

"I do not, but I believe in bumping grates, and I mean to discover the cause."

There was no fire in the grate, so I got down on my hands and knees and stuck my head up the flue, using a candle to give me a light. I saw a great deal of soot, some quantity of which brushed loose and landed on my hair, but I discovered nothing of interest. "I'll go down in the basement and have a look," I decided.

"Wait till morning," Slack advised.

"The house may fall on our heads before morning. I'll go now, but if you are afraid, Slack, perhaps George will accompany me."

George looked more frightened than Slack, to tell the truth, but was not about to admit before two ladies that he was afraid of ghosts, and with an unsteady hand he took up a candelabrum and came with me.

I am not afraid of ghosts, nor the dark, nor of long shadows stretching along gloomy passages, but I am not entirely insensitive, and I admit the atmosphere was eerie. It was also — I grasp in vain for the proper word. I could *almost* swear I heard sounds behind the wall on which the grate was located. Sounds of movement, and once what might even have been human voices. The grate is situated on the east wall of Hillcrest, the wall that faces Belview. That particular wall is entirely different from the others in the cellar. It is made of stone, beautifully cut, fitted, really a work of art. The other walls are of irregular stone, and on one side the wall is just plain dirt for the bottom two feet. There is no shaft going from grate to cellar, for easier cleaning of the ashes. The ashes have to be swept from the hearth abovestairs each day. I had already noticed this feature and found it a little inconvenient, but then not every grate has a shaft going to the cellar, so that was not unusual. The stone wall was extremely solid. There was not a single sign of loose work that might have moved involuntarily. The trouble was not in this area, and before long George and I were retreating rather hastily up the stairs, stumbling over ourselves and each other in our eagerness to get away.

"Everything is firm downstairs. The trouble must be outside, in the chimney," I told Slack.

Glancing to her, I observed that while George and I had done the investigating, it was Slack who was trembling, her face chalk white. "I heard voices!" she declared in a hollow voice. "The place is *haunted*, Priscilla."

"Nonsense! You don't believe in ghosts, and neither do I. If you heard voices, you heard human voices. Mine and George's very likely."

"No, they were deep men's voices," she insisted.

George took no umbrage at this, nor had he the right to. His voice is high, and in fact we said very little to each other while in the cellar.

"Come outside, George, and let us see if there is someone prowling about," I said to him.

George licked his lips, and they discovered a new position — terror. The bottom one hung slack and trembling. "Oh, now, Priscilla, you don't want to go out on such a night as this."

"It is not cold and not raining. I *do* want to go out. Do you refuse to come with me? Slack, as George is afraid of his own shadow, perhaps *you* . . ."

"No, no, I ain't afraid," George said, quite obviously lying. "The thing is, it might be the Gentlemen, you — know."

"Smugglers!" Slack goggled, and took a step backward into her chair.

"We have a saying hereabouts," George told us. "'Watch the wall, my darling.' Turn your head the other way, in other words, and see and hear nothing when the Gentlemen are about. That way you will come to no harm. They don't like interfering with."

"Neither do *I* like interfering with my grate. Do you come or not, George?" I took up a candle as I spoke, to show him I meant to go, alone, if necessary.

"Yes, yes, I'll go with you, but we don't want a light. We'll slip out the back way and go quietly forward without being seen. There's no thinking we can stop them, Priscilla. If we see anything, I'll nip into town and report it to the revenue officer."

I was not afraid but am not quite a fool either, I hope, and agreed to his plan. We went out the kitchen door, eased our way silently around the house to the front, and saw absolutely nothing. No sound or sign disturbed the calm of a late night in summer. The moon shone, an owl hooted hauntingly from some faraway tree, and in the distance the ocean lapped peacefully.

"Let us see if there are boats at the seaside," I suggested. We have a view of the ocean from my house front, but not of the shore. It is necessary to cross the road and walk a couple of yards to the top of the embankment and look down. There was no boat, nobody there at all. The beach was totally deserted. In some mystification, and also some relief, we returned home rather quickly.

Slack sat waiting for us, on the anxious seat.

"Nothing. There was no one there," I told her, and she breathed a sigh of relief.

"I'd prefer a ghost to a smuggler," she said.

We had a glass of wine to calm our nerves (I had long since augmented the dozen bottles in the cellar), discussed the matter in the fruitless fashion in which mysteries must always be discussed, and finally began hinting George away. He usually tumbles to a hint very readily, for the truth is he enjoys these social calls no more than do I; but on this occasion he was reluctant to leave, and the reason, I suspected, was plain and simple fear to go out alone.

Slack suggested he take my carriage and two foot-boys for the half-mile drive, and he snatched at it.

Really, I hardly blamed him. We went to bed with our heads full of smugglers, Slack to dream of them, I with a decision to discover of Officer Smith, our local revenueman, just how great a threat they constituted.

The next morning gave me a foretaste of how bleak and dreary it can be on the Atlantic coast in autumn. It was not yet into really bad weather, but Nature threw up at summer's end a day that reeked of autumn. It was raining hard, grey sheets driven by a raucous gale from the ocean, causing the drops to slap the window-panes with a driving force. No lesson on Juliette was possible today. I had determined I would have another, the knee notwithstanding. All plans for the day were cancelled perforce. Slack and I sat huddled before the grate in the Blue Saloon, with our faces and fronts too hot from the flames and our backs chilled by the draughts from the windows. In mid-morning we had candles lit to lighten the gloom. Really, it was remarkably uncomfortable. I half wished I had not rejected Clavering's offer out of hand. I held a book in my hands but did not read; Slack held her knitting and did knit.

"The only thing to be said for this day is that George will not come to call," I said a little petulantly. It was eleven o'clock, an hour which frequently saw him at our door. No sooner were the words out of my mouth than the knocker sounded.

"Maybe something happened last night on the way home," Slack said with a smile. She was always happy to welcome him.

"If anything had happened, I trust my footboys would have told us when they returned," I pointed out.

The caller proved not to be George but an even less welcome one, the Duke of Clavering. I recognized his deep voice as he handed his coat and hat to the butler, saying, "Looks like autumn's here, eh?" in an abominably cheerful tone.

He must have moved swiftly, for before the butler could announce him he strode in, rubbing his hands together and smiling. "Good morning, ladies. Nice day."

We both surveyed him with hostile eyes. He ought to have realized he was not welcome, but he was one of those people with elephant-like hides. He advanced to the fire and drew up a chair for himself between us. "How is the sprained knee going on?" he asked me.

"Sprained knee?" I enquired, as though the matter had slipped my mind. "Oh, you refer to the incident yesterday."

"Yes, the spill you took from Juliette."

"I had forgotten all about it. My knee is fine, thank you."

"Good."

"In fact, I had been looking forward to another ride today, but the weather, of course, makes it impossible. I am surprised to find anyone out in such a gale."

He did not take the hint and explain what brought him out, but said instead, "Autumn is come. This is typical autumn weather here on the coast. You will become inured to it if you stay."

"There is no question of my not staying."

"Ah, then you like the rain. That is good. We get a great deal of it."

"We always got a deal of rain in Wiltshire," I replied.

"Of course, the winds here make the rain more unpleasant. A very driving rain we get, and cold."

"Particularly inclement weather for an invalid with lung trouble I should think," I replied, letting him know I understood very well the direction of his talk. He was painting a glum picture to encourage me to sell.

He made no reply to this, but the flash of comprehension from his dark eyes told me he had understood my remark.

He glanced around the room to give himself time to think of another tactic and said at length, "I see you have redone the draperies, very nice."

"Thank you."

"A pity the way everything deteriorates so quickly here on the coast. Those lovely rose velvet hangings will be faded to grey in a year's time. The sun and salt air combined are very hard on them."

"We had the same difficulty in Wiltshire, don't you remember, Slack?" I asked. "But there it was the sun and dust that did the mischief. We had to change the draperies very frequently."

"Every year," Slack seconded me. For a moment there I feared she meant to fail me, for she is really honest almost to a fault. She had no more love for Clavering than I had myself, however. She would have been glad enough for me to sell, but the Duke was an arrogant, aggressive man, and thus she had taken him in dislike.

He gave up trying to outdo us on bad weather and turned to other disadvantages of the area. "I hope the road isn't flooded with this downpour. It happens every spring. The road is always washed out for a month with the high tides and rain. This low-lying land you are situated on is the worst, of course. Up on the hill at Belview it doesn't trouble us." Actually we, too, were on a little hill, but Belview was higher.

"How nice! We shall have to set up a yacht, Slack. I always wanted to do some boating. We were landlocked at Wiltshire."

"You certainly must make some arrangement for the month or so you will be cut off. Get in supplies, have your livestock removed, set up an emergency station, and so on."

"The spring is a long way off yet."

"Oh, yes, we are just getting into the bitter autumn and winter weather now. Half a year of wind and lashing rains ahead of us. I daresay your first month here gave you a very misleading picture of the place. In the summer months it is lively and pleasant on the coast, with all the visitors from London and sunshine and so on. The winter is long and bleak."

"I did not particularly enjoy the crowds of visitors. I look forward to the peace and quiet. We are not the sort, Slack and I, who enjoy a mass of milling strangers at our doorstep but will do very well with our few friends."

"Not much to do all winter long, of course. You will have read the two dozen books at the circulating library by then, and the assemblies in Pevensey are cancelled every winter."

"I gave up attending assemblies some years ago, about the same time I began buying books. You were not particularly looking forward to them, were you Slack?" I asked in an ironic vein.

Slack gave no verbal reply but only smirked on Clavering to show him that she, too, understand what he was up to. He sat on unoffended and undismayed, racking his brain for other levers to pry us loose.

"Have you had any trouble with smugglers at all?" he asked, to draw our attention to yet another coastal plague. No mild "Gentlemen" for him; he wanted to make them sound as blood-curdling as possible.

"No. That is . . ." I stopped, and he looked up quickly with interest. I related the episode of the banging grate, making it a sort of interesting phenomenon, or joke.

"It sounds as though you've been visited by smugglers all right," he told us, with the greatest relish.

"I can't think so, unless they were phantom smugglers. There wasn't a sign of a boat on the beach."

"You weren't foolish enough to leave the house when they were around!" he shouted, as though it were only by the sheerest of luck I lived to tell it. "You never want to do that. It is courting disaster. Anyway, they wouldn't leave the stuff out in full view — or the boats either. It was probably landed some nights ago and has been stored on your property to be transferred later."

"They surely wouldn't be so bold as to hide it on my land without permission!"

"Permission!" He threw back his head and went off into a roar of mirth out of all proportion to the humour of the remark. "My dear Miss Denver, the smugglers don't ask permission. They are a law unto themselves, do exactly as they wish; and if you are wise, you won't trouble them. They are very vicious. As to you two women living alone here in such an ideal spot for them to bring the brandy ashore, there in the cove at your doorstep ... Really, you don't want to make any trouble for them, or you will certainly suffer reprisals."

"I shall report it to the revenue officer. I had planned to do so today, but the rain kept me home."

"What, this little shower? You must get used to that. It is nothing out of the ordinary. This is one of the better days we are likely to see before next spring."

"When the *floods* set in!" I added. "I understand you very well, Your Grace. You are painting the most lugubrious picture possible to get me to change my mind about selling Hillcrest."

"Seaview!"

"Hillcrest! It is *my* home, and I shall call it what I wish. I do not plan to leave. In fairness to your invalid aunt, I must tell you that you had better find some other cold, windswept, flooded spot for her to recuperate in."

"Thirty-five hundred," he said.

For a moment I did not understand him. He went on, "I'll raise the price to thirty-five hundred. It is a better than fair offer. You won't match it elsewhere."

"I don't intend to sell."

"It's my top offer, and more than the place is worth."

"Why do you offer more than it's worth?"

"*It's mine*! That is — do you have a pen and I'll show you what I mean." Slack got the pen and paper, and Clavering drew up a pie-shaped wedge. His hand moved swiftly and purposefully, the emerald not winking today in the dim light. "This is Clavering land," he said. "And this is Seaview." He took a bite out of the end of the piece of pie and decorated it with an S (for Seaview, I assumed).

"This land has been in the family for five hundred years. You can see Seaview is an integral part of my holdings. I wish to restore it. It ruins the outline."

This must have sounded a paltry excuse, even to himself. "As I mentioned, I have plans for it. It has very meaningful associations, family associations, for me. It was built by my great-grandfather from stone taken from Clavering land, a fallen chapel. Every stone and piece of wood in it has meaning for me. The woodwork, the carved panelling, actually comes from Belview, done by Grinling Gibbons. It means a great deal to me."

"It means a great deal to me as well," I informed him, unimpressed by his claims of fine family feelings. He was merely greedy, wanted to add another house to his collection.

"What can it possibly mean to you? You haven't been here above a month. The weather is bad, the smugglers will annoy you, you are cut off from society. There is nothing to recommend the place to any normal person."

"My aunt lives less than a mile away."

"Another disadvantage, I think?" he asked with a mocking smile.

"Not in the least. I am very fond of my aunt and cousin," I said blightingly.

"Tell me, did you make good your threat to wring her neck?"

"All families have their little disagreements from time to time. The matter is settled between us."

"Now, look, you could buy yourself a very fine home in Pevensey for the price I am offering you. A better house than this, and with your own land. You would still be close enough to visit Lady Inglewood, if that is now considered an advantage."

"Why can't *you* understand I don't want to sell my house? You just want to set mantraps around Seaview, too, to keep anyone from disturbing your tranquility on those rare occasions when you are home. You will find us unobtrusive neighbours, sir. Don't fear we mean to pester you."

"I meant to warn you about the mantraps. Lucky you didn't fall into one yesterday. It is the reason I came, to inform you of them."

"Very well, I am informed, and will stay out of your spinney."

"Actually the spinney is safe enough. It is the meadow just beyond that is particularly well trapped. I wish to keep trespassers out of it."

"You will not be troubled with Miss Slack or me trespassing in your meadow, spinney, or anywhere else."

"It is because of the Roman ruins, you see."

"So I have heard."

"May I know where you heard?"

"My cousin, Lord Inglewood, told me."

"I see. I don't know what he might have told you. He is not at all interested in the matter. The fact is, my family chapel was built over a Roman temple. It in turn was destroyed a few centuries ago, and it was only in the fairly recent past that we discovered the temple ruins beneath. I am toying with the idea of having it restored as a temple — many of the original stones are still there. The remainder were hauled off by some fellow who took the notion he would use them for a dry wall, hence the traps."

I listened with only a small interest to this. I had been thinking for the past few moments I ought to offer the Duke some refreshment. He was an unpleasant and obnoxious man who came here to harass us, but he was a duke, and I did wish to get my lease renewed, so at this point I enquired if he would take a glass of wine, thinking to mention five hundred pounds, as my aunt had suggested.

"The rain's letting up. I think I'd better be off," he replied.

"Letting up so soon, is it? I thought that as in the Bible, we could expect forty days and forty nights of uninterrupted downpour. I had half decided to commission an ark and start collecting pairs of the local fauna. The coast is not living up to its reputation. Why, do you know, I think I see a ray of sun trying to push through."

"Come the deluge, you are welcome to berth on my yacht, Miss Denver. I have not yet collected my female

Homo sapiens. I wouldn't want to set sail without that important species." He lifted a heavy black brow and arose. "A delightful visit. May I return?"

"Certainly. Any time you find yourself caught in one of our local typhoons, feel free to seek shelter at Hillcrest. You will find no mantraps between the road and the front door. We are not so inhospitable as some of our neighbours."

"There are no traps in the spinney. You may feel free to ride there, Miss Denver, but I hope you will not ride unescorted, for your own safety. And you really ought to get a tamer mount, too."

"I like a spirited animal."

"But can you handle one?" he asked, and looked a challenge at me. Somehow, I had the impression it was the human animal before me we were speaking of, and not Juliette.

"I am not easily cowed, Your Grace. Wilkins will see you out."

He bowed, rather nimbly for a large hulk of a man, and left.

It was not till he was gone that I discovered a few traces of confusion in his story. How did it come that my house had been built with stones from his fallen chapel, that some of those same stones had been stolen by a neighbour, and still sufficient remained that he meant to reconstruct the temple that had stood there in Roman times? It seemed an overaccounting for them. Then, too, he would get his land back in nineteen years — why was he so anxious to do it *now* that he would pay me more than the place was worth for it? If it was no more than the tip bit off his piece of pie, he could wait nineteen years. And if he couldn't wait, why had he not offered the deal to my aunt, who would certainly have jumped at his extravagant offer? No, while the place stood empty he didn't begrudge the bite out of his pie. What he wished to do was to get rid of *me*, to have no one to disturb him and his mantraps. Did he take me for an interfering woman because I had ridden in his spinney without permission? But he had said specifically he didn't mind that — I might feel free to ride in it. The more I considered the matter the more confused I became, and the more determined to remain exactly where I was and see what happened. And it was not too long before things began happening.

CHAPTER
FOUR

The storm's fury was spent by lunchtime, and by early afternoon the sun was shining. All the bleak greyness was gone out of the day, and the breeze from the windows was refreshing rather than chilling.

"Slack, I'm going into Pevensey to speak to the revenue officer," I announced. "Will you come with me?"

The question was rhetorical. Slack is an inveterate gadabout. She had on her pelisse and bonnet five minutes before I was ready myself, and I am not a laggard. The road was wet, of course, but to speak of flooding was absurd. In fact, as I noticed the road had a good high shoulder, and as no one else had so much as mentioned spring flooding to me, I assumed it was one of Clavering's exaggerations to make the place sound unattractive. I soon found the threat of smugglers to have been similarly overstated.

Officer Smith was in charge of the customs in the area, and it was to his little office next door the milliner's that I sought him out to report the strange sounds heard the night before.

"I can't think it was smugglers, ma'am," he assured me. "There is little enough smuggling going forth at

55

this time, and what there is comes in at Romney Marsh up the east coast for the most part. Since the war with Napoleon, smuggling is cut down considerably. A mite dangerous for the lads to be plying the Channel in these perilous times, to say nothing of *landing* in France."

"You don't think they might have been using Seaview for hiding their contraband, then? Its having stood empty for a while might have led them to think it a safe spot." I felt the name Hillcrest might confuse him, because of McCurdy's. Actually I would have to get busy and find another name.

"Mercy, ma'am, you've been there upward of a month, now. If there ever was anything there, it would be long gone. There are plenty of safer places about, abandoned barns or buildings, ditches, hayricks and so on, and plenty of people that are willing to look the other way for the price of a little of the goods. Why, it isn't in the least necessary for them to risk putting it on occupied land without permission. You, between a pair of lords as you are, are in the safest spot on the coast. You may be sure they'd never land it on Clavering's doorstep. Seaview is too close to His Grace for them to be monkeying about there. They know he takes a dim view of it. Why, it wouldn't be much of an exaggeration to say he does as much patrolling as I do myself. Many's the time I've seen His Grace out in his yacht, in the summer, you know, when he's in residence at Belview, tailing suspicious vessels. He keeps a patrol on his whole stretch of coast, has men posted to see no one lands. You couldn't be safer if you were in a church."

"It was the Duke of Clavering who suggested to me the noises I heard might be smugglers," I told him.

"Did he do so? That surprises me, for if anyone knows how unlikely it is they'd come in at Seaview, it is His Grace. Still, he has a kind of a mania about them. Sees smugglers in his sleep and imagines them around every corner."

"He felt that as Miss Slack and I have no man about the house, except for the servants, of course, they might impose on us."

"Ah, well, they'd never harm a lady in any case, so you've nothing to fear. They're not vicious at all. They will have their little joke. Once stuck my head into a rabbit burrow and drove a T stake between my legs to prevent my getting out, but that's the worst I've heard of them doing recently." This sounded bad enough to me.

"I've kept my eyes open, and I'd say since catching the fellows last week, there's only one ship operating here nowadays. And it isn't a regular one either. But I keep a sharp eye on it, you may be sure. I'll stop in next time I'm out Seaview way and have a look around. But there's nowhere there to hide it. You haven't a real farm, just your bit of a barn for the horses, with no big ricks nor a good deep ditch nor a thing. You've no fuel house, no potato graves, apple-loft and your hedgerows is only three yards long. Why, it would surely be found if they were foolish enough to try to hide it there. Let me know if you have any more trouble, but it seems to me your noise was no more than a couple of poachers."

"They would not poach Clavering's land, all trapped and posted as it is."

"No, not Clavering's. People steer a wide path of Belview. It was your cousin's place I was thinking of. Inglewood is considered fair game. Gets more than its share, because of no one daring to set a foot on Clavering's land. It might be they were running from Inglewood and got a scare by Clavering's warden. They'd be at pains to hide their bag — might have chucked it under some bushes or whatnot at your place."

"I suppose it might have been that," I said, dissatisfied. "But it was the *grate* that made the racket, and that suggests someone right *in* the house."

"It's odd, surely. If you find out what it was, let me know, and in any case I'll stop around next time I'm out that way."

We returned home, had a call from my aunt before dinner to enquire into the grate and to be assured that it was only the house settling. She suggested it was the first fire of the season that accounted for it, with the metal chimney-lining expanding, and it was a clever idea except that the fire hadn't been lit. Still, she talked it down as nothing, and in the end I felt I had been rash to go dashing into town speaking of smugglers. She confirmed Smith's story that she had never seen a sign nor heard a word of a smuggler along our coastline, due to Clavering's patrols. She laid to rest as well my fears of spring flooding and six months of steady rain. The road had flooded once twenty years ago for a few days, and never since. It had been raised a foot at that time, and resurfaced since, so Clavering's dire warnings were intended only to frighten us.

"He is extremely disagreeable, Priscilla. You don't want to have a thing to do with him," she added.

This surprised me, for the Claverings were a very old family of impeccable, indeed illustrious, lineage. And he was a duke; this should have appealed to her love of old and mighty blood, tinged with gold, too, to judge by his lands and home.

"He never has a soul to Belview," she said next, which explained the acid remark. He had nothing to do with her, so to save face she said she had nothing to do with him.

"He has been here twice," I pointed out, and watched her bridle.

"He only wants to get Seaview from you. He might have told *me* he wanted to buy it. I would not have been averse to selling it to him."

"He has upped the price to thirty-five hundred," I had the exquisite joy of telling her. She was desolate now that she had never approached him. I could see her writhe in chagrin.

"I'm sure it's worth every penny of it. Naturally I made a very good price for my own niece." The thing was done, and the only way now was to accept it with good grace and prate of generosity.

"What can he want with it?" she asked. "To pay thirty-five hundred pounds, and it is to revert to him, the *land*, I mean, in nineteen years. I think he must have run mad."

George was sent over in the evening to entertain us, which he did by routing through the shelves for an old copy of *The Sporting Magazine* left behind by Mr Seymour and poking his head into it while Slack and I set up the tambour frame to make a firescreen. I was coming to see that if the windows were to admit two-thirds of every wind that blew past, our backs would require some protection. With memories of his experience the night before, George left early. As soon as I suggested having a fire lit, in fact. The grate gave another performance, but in much diminished form. I took the notion that on this occasion it was indeed having the fire lit that caused the sounds. I hoped that with successive lightings whatever was bumping would get knocked into a position where it no longer rattled, and we would have peace.

Perusing these pages, I see I have omitted many personages in our life. We had other acquaintances than my relations, the Duke of Clavering, and the revenue officer. Neighbours came to call often, and we returned their calls. A few card parties and dinners had been attended, and three teas had been given by us. We had a quite respectable number of people to bow and speak to in the village, and never left the church without being drawn into some group for a chat after service on Sundays. Both Slack and I were active with the women of the parish in visiting the sick, feeding the hungry, and clothing the naked (in a Christian sense, of course). Without boasting, I think it only just to mention that other gentlemen than Cousin George took some little interest in me, too. There was a certain Mr Harkness who . . . However, that has nothing to do with my story. One of our favourite callers was Mr Harvey McMaster, a gentleman farmer nearby who was well educated, well-to-do, and well mannered.

It was Slack's unpleasant custom to refer to him as my "beau," which was an exaggeration, though I did enjoy his company. He was well over thirty-five and plain in appearance. Some few days previously he had been to call and asked me to accompany him to Eastbourne, where he had to go on business. I had been looking forward to the trip, but when the actual day dawned fine, clear, and bright, I was a little sorry I was to be deprived of my second attempt at riding Juliette. I feared she would take the notion she had bested me and was to spend the remainder of her days standing in the stable, eating her head off. However, I had accepted the invitation and would, of course, go with him. I had not said, but thought, that he would take his closed carriage and Slack would accompany us. She had on her black suit for the trip and was quite put out to observe he drove up in his sporting curricle that held only two.

"We can take my carriage," I told her.

"Oh, no, your beau has purposely brought his curricle to get you alone. Don't let *me* interfere with his plans."

"Don't be an ass, Slack."

"Don't worry about me. I'll call on Lady Ing instead. She is lending me a pattern for a netted shawl. I'll have need of it before long, I think."

"Suit yourself. You're welcome to come if you wish."

"Mr McMaster will not welcome me."

Her coyness deprived her of the trip, and I would have liked her company nearly as much as she would have liked coming with us. She must be taught to curb these sly taunts about Mr McMaster, however, and leaving her behind was the surest way to do it.

The trip was enjoyable without her. It was my first longish trip in an open carriage — Mr McMaster had driven me home from Pevensey once before. There is nothing like a high-perch open carriage to give a view of the countryside, though, of course, both wind and dust are included in the trip. Contrary to Slack's teasing, the conversation throughout was most decorous, not a word spoken that the bishop could frown at. I told him something about the part of Wiltshire where I had been raised, and he in turn explained his home territory to me. This south-east corner of England, he informed me as we drove along, was the most history-laden part of the country. It was here the Celts had landed, and been pushed off by the Anglo-Saxons. The Normans, he assured me, though their conquest is thought of in terms of Hastings, had actually landed at Pevensey Bay, right on our doorstep. The Spanish Armada hadn't made it to shore, but this was the spot they had their eye on. And at this very moment Napoleon coveted our shores. Mr McMaster pointed out architectural features denoting the reigns of the various invaders. A Roman fort, a Norman church, a modern Martello Tower built to hold Boney at bay.

"Bonaparte is not likely to invade us now, when he is busy with Prussia, do you think?" I asked.

"You will notice the Martello Towers are manned," he pointed out, and indeed sentries were to be seen in their highly visible red jackets, parading back and forth before the grey stone cylindrical towers that spanned the coast at regular intervals. "Behind the slits of the windows, glasses are trained on the sea twenty-four hours a day," he added.

"There is little enough to see."

"Best to be prepared. Boney might think this is an excellent time for a surprise attack on us, when we assume he is busy at Prussia. Of course, he is fighting there, and doing pretty well, too, winning at Lutzen, but there is no saying he hasn't an army preparing at Calais or Boulogne to slip across La Manche one foggy night and attack us. I know I keep my blunderbuss loaded and have my men trained up as well as ever they were in Papa's day, when invasion was considered imminent."

At Wilton, a safe hundred and fifty miles from this attack-prone coast, no mention of invasion from Bonaparte had been made for years; but, of course, he was feared, dreaded, and those round stone towers brought forcibly home the reality that he was still a powerful foe. I felt a little icy finger of fear creep up my spine at this talk. This was more likely to put me off with my new home than any talk of smugglers or floods. Odd Clavering hadn't thought to mention this particular menace to me. I brought up the subject of smugglers, just to gauge the sentiments of an objective, sensible person like McMaster. Clearly Clavering had been trying to frighten me, but possibly Officer Smith painted a rosier picture than was true. He was in charge and would like to give the impression he had things under control.

"Oh, yes, they are still active," he told me, without a moment's hesitation.

"I have heard that in wartime they do less smuggling because France is not safe for them."

"Ever since Boney went to Prussia, it has been going on much as it used to. Englishmen don't stop drinking brandy and buying silk only because of a war."

"The majority of it comes ashore at Romney, I understand."

"Most of it, for the landing is easier there, and concealment, too, but from Margate to Bournemouth there are men engaged in it. We have some right here in Pevensey."

"Officer Smith keeps a close eye on them, I should think."

"He does what he can, but he's no Argus with a hundred eyes. He took a boatload a week or so ago, but there is collusion between them, of course."

"The revenuemen let them through for a price, you mean?"

"They have clamped down pretty heavily on that. There was some scandal of one fellow, Lazy Louie they call him, who had the revenuemen from Romney to Pevensey on the take, and they dismissed the officers. It amazes me that Lazy Louie walks the streets a free man this day. Bribed the judge, I suppose," he said, laughing.

"What did you mean by collusion, then, if the practice has been stopped?"

"You must know the smugglers are in an excellent position to do a little spying for England. Who but they would know if Boney is assembling a flotilla at Boulogne? Some of them are spies as well as smugglers, with a gentleman's agreement that they will not be caught, I think. They do a great deal of good in their former capacity and little enough harm in the latter if you don't bother them. The government is taxing us to death. Ten percent on our income wasn't enough, they had to raise it for the war; and a guinea a head for male servants, a tax on our carriages and our windows and I don't know what else. They could at least let a man have a glass of brandy without paying through the nose for it. I don't buy smuggled brandy myself, but I drink it. A little, I mean — I don't blink an eye if a friend offers me a glass of brandy. I know it is smuggled, but I don't resent it, and it is no secret every inch of silk at Peters' Drapery Shop is smuggled."

My mind flew to my green silk gown, and I felt that I, too, was an unwitting accessory to the Gentlemen.

"Well, half the men doing it are so poor it is all that is keeping body and soul together," he went on. "With the common lands enclosed they have nowhere to graze a cow, and with fellows like Clavering trapping their land so that even a hare is beyond them, what are they to do? Of course they can fish. We on the coast can at least depend on cheap and ready food from the sea."

We arrived at Eastbourne, a quaintly formal little place, rather elegant in appearance. McMaster went to the grain merchant, and I poked about the shops for an hour, meeting him for lunch at an inn. It was a trifle chilly on the way home. Quite a brisk breeze blew in from the ocean, and when we got to Hillcrest, I asked him in for tea. Slack was on her high ropes at having been abandoned. She had not gone to visit Lady Inglewood, after all, but had sat home the whole time to make me feel guilty.

She succeeded only in making me angry. "Cut off your nose to spite your face if you like," I told her, after McMaster had taken his tea and left us. In retaliation she kept from me a note that had been delivered at our door shortly after my departure. This was not given over to me till an hour after dinner, when we were sitting by the grate where we had again laid a fire. No rattling had followed the lighting, and I assumed it was at an end.

"Oh, this note came for you after you left," she told me then and handed me an envelope bearing a crest. I am morally certain she hadn't forgotten it for a moment but kept it back for spite.

"Kind of you to bother giving it to me," I replied, mistaking it for my aunt's stationery. Naturally, Aunt Ethelberta used nothing but crested paper. In fact, the ugly Inglewood crest designed by some totally unaesthetic person adorned many of her belongings. But this was not her crest. I did not recognize it at once, but as I was acquainted with only one other titled person, I had a fair idea it was from Clavering, as indeed it was.

"If it is an offer to purchase Hillcrest, I will pitch it straight into the grate," I said angrily.

It was not an offer to purchase. It was a bare two lines scrawled in black ink in a fist that managed to be both casual and arrogant. The two lines filled the card, as Clavering's black presence filled a room. "Please come to tea tomorrow at four o'clock," it said, and was signed "Clavering." Not your obedient servant, or yours truly, or anything but "Clavering." Blunt to the point of rudeness. He could make even a social invitation an insult.

"You should have given it to me sooner and I could have sent in our refusal," I told her, handing the note along to her.

"Refusal? Will you not accept?"

"Certainly not. This is no invitation; it is a summons."

"I'd like to see Belview. It looks very interesting from what I can glimpse through the trees."

"We would be overset by mantraps along the road, I fancy. I shall not accept." She returned the card, and I flung it into the flames.

"Lady Inglewood says he asks no one there," she began, trying to tempt me.

"Which means he does not ask her."

"It would be fun to go to spite her."

"What a petty mind you hide behind that pious face, Slack. I'm ashamed of you. Well, I suppose I can't reply before tomorrow. I don't intend sending my servants out into the night."

"You might change your mind."

I saw Slack was eager to go. I was curious to see Belview myself but would not accept a summons. "My mind is made up."

We discussed the trip to Eastbourne, and I painted a rosy picture to give Slack an idea what she had missed by her sullen temper.

"It seems I am not to go to Eastbourne and not to go to Belview. I might as well take to my bed, for it seems I am to go nowhere of any interest!"

"You go to visit Belview if you think it is your company he seeks. But pray don't sell Hillcrest out from under me. That is what this invitation is all about."

"I know it, but we could go without selling the house."

The knocker sounded. It was nine o'clock in the evening. If George came in the morning, he came at eleven; if in the evening, at nine. I assumed we were to have the pleasure of looking at the back of whatever magazine he chose to read this evening, and waited for his shuffling entry. The firm tread on the hallway floor told me it was not George even before the deep voice spoke. "Evening, Wilkins. Are the ladies at home?"

It was Clavering, come in person for a reply to his invitation. He was certainly eager to buy my house. The evening took an unexpected turn. Slack found herself a beau, but I shall write all about it in the next chapter. It deserves its own, and I am too fagged to do it justice at this time.

CHAPTER
FIVE

Clavering waited to be announced on this occasion, adopting formal manners to match his attire. He wore black evening clothes, jacket, and pantaloons. I surmised he had been out to dinner, but was incorrect.

"I have just seen the last of my guests home and took the liberty of dropping in to see if you had my invitation," he said, helping himself to a chair with a mere vestige of a bow, a ducking of the head really toward us both in turn.

If he had been seeing guests home, I took for granted they were female guests and felt some little anger that he invited us to tea, others to dinner. I had placed little reliance on my aunt's statement that he did not entertain. Certainly a man in his position must entertain lavishly.

"Yes, I just received it this moment. Miss Slack forgot to give it to me earlier. I was out all day. Very kind of you to offer, but I'm afraid we are busy tomorrow."

"All day? We could make it a morning visit, if that is more convenient for you."

"Yes, all day," I said firmly.

"And the evening? Are you free for dinner?"

"We are dining out," I lied amiably. Slack told me later I used a very spiteful tone of voice, but that was only her anger at my rejecting all his offers.

"How busy you manage to make yourself in this quiet little backwater. Morning, noon, and night."

"Quite so. Taking advantage of the good weather while it lasts, you know, and the roads are passable."

Slack's temper came to the boil and then boiled over. "We could cancel tea with Lady Inglewood very easily," she informed me.

We had no plans for tea with my aunt, no plans of any sort, but this she considered would force me to accept Clavering's invitation. "I wouldn't like to do that," I told her with a repressive stare.

"Surely she would forgive you. You are neighbours. You might visit her any time; I am here only for a few days and would like to see you at Belview," Clavering said.

I felt a little pang then at my refusal. Really I was very curious to see Belview, and if he would soon be leaving, when might we have another opportunity? I sat undecided, and silent.

"I should think you would be interested to see it, since it is the model of your own home. I had thought to give you a tour of the house. It has some interesting features — a Marine Room with a good collection of shells, and some quite intriguing Roman artifacts."

"Well, perhaps . . ." I said, intercepting a vigorous nod from Slack.

"Your aunt will not mind in the least. It's settled you come to tea at four o'clock," Clavering said in a very

70

high-handed manner, then turned immediately to other topics. "As you were away all day, I assumed you did not ride at all?"

"No, I drove over to Eastbourne with Mr McMaster. It seems a charming city."

"They have a fair museum," he answered. I had not seen it, nor heard that it possessed such a place.

"What sort of museum?" Slack asked.

"Oh, a Roman museum, of course," he answered, as though there were no other kind. "About your grate, Miss Denver, has it ceased troubling you with its noise?"

"Yes, it has been very good lately. Not a sound out of it today. I think it has settled down and am very happy, for we have checked everything from cellar to chimney and can't see what should be causing it. We were half afraid of ghosts."

"You believe in ghosts?" he asked, in quite a polite voice.

"Certainly not. It was a joke, though it was a very odd noise all the same."

"I could swear I heard *voices* when you were in the cellar," Slack said.

"Where did they come from? What part of the room?" Clavering asked as he arose and walked to the grate. It was Slack who kept speaking about voices. I wished she would let the matter drop, or he'd take us for a pair of nervous spinsters, but, no, she joined him and tried to decide from behind which stone the voices had come.

"It seemed to be more on this side," she said, pointing to the right-hand side. The fireplace is on the east wall, facing Clavering's land, as I believe I mentioned earlier. The south wall faces the sea and is all windowed. In the corner between the fireplace and front wall there is a large, nicely carved parson's bench with a high back. The room is panelled three-quarters of the way to the ceiling, and the bench blends in perfectly with it, being of the same wood and carved in the same manner, with a trefoil design repeated three times at the top of the arched panels, to fill in the point. I have often seen such a design in the pews of old Gothic churches.

"The fireplace itself or the bench?" Clavering asked.

I felt he was making a deal too much of her foolish imaginings, and perhaps he knew it, too, for Slack tells me I have acquired a revolting way of twitching my shoulders and pursing my lips at such times of displeasure. If this description is true; and I sincerely hope it is not, I say in my own defence it is a mannerism I picked up from herself. One I always considered the peculiar prerogative of old maids and had determined to avoid.

"A bit in between," she informed him, and walked to his side. Now I have told you Slack dislikes men, especially masculine men, whereas she occasionally takes a shine to a man-milliner like George, what Papa would have called a "skirter." Yet another facet of her personality has not been shown. It is about to reveal itself now. *I* think she dislikes real men because she thinks they hate her, or are laughing at her, or some such thing. Only let them show a jot more than the minimum of politeness and she falls under their spell like the veriest schoolgirl with her Italian dancing master. I could see in her pleased glances at Clavering that if I didn't watch her closely, she would begin touting him up to me as an excellent fellow.

"This is nonsense," I said firmly, and refused to leave my chair to join them in the search for the echo of an echo.

They both ignored me. "Maybe more from the wall than the grate," I heard Slack say next, and she began glancing along the panelled wall, as though the imaginary sound may have left a visible trace. And Clavering, who was certainly up to something, went right along with her foolishness, tapping panels and putting his ear to the wall for hollow sounds.

"It was the metal in the chimney expanding with the heat," I said.

"The fire wasn't lit the first time," Slack reminded me. "Could it have come from the bench, I wonder," she went on, enjoying very much showing me she had Clavering's attention. Oh, yes, he would be a paragon before she went to bed that night. If he went much further, she'd be trying to tell me the swarthy old gypsy was handsome.

"Maybe if we moved the bench away from the wall . . ." she said, already placing her hands on one end to assist the Duke of Clavering to move my furniture about, and likely discover a roll of dust and a ridge of grime behind it.

"It doesn't move. It's built in," he told her.

I don't know why it should have annoyed me so much that *he* knew things about my house I didn't know myself. "Nonsense, of course it moves," I heard myself say. And *I* was the one who wanted this folly stopped.

He didn't say a word but lifted his black brows at me and put his two hands around the corners of it and began pulling and heaving. It was awkward to get a good hold on it, because it went right to the floor; it was not on feet.

"All right. Please stop before you pull it loose from the wall!" I said angrily, for it was perfectly plain that if that ox couldn't budge it, it didn't budge.

"Really, I think the voices came from a place closer to the fire-place," Slack then said, unwilling to have her moment of glory shortened.

"I begin to think they emanated from your head, Slack," I said. She had become so infatuated with her new beau that she didn't bother to reply, but only smiled at Clavering in a way that said as clear as day, I must humour the moonling.

Clavering too decided to humour me, and they both took a seat. "Well, I believe the Duke has earned a glass of wine, Priscilla," Slack told me.

"I hope a guest in my house doesn't have to earn a glass of wine by rearranging my furniture," I said, quite curtly, and she was off with a swish of her black skirts to get not only wine but macaroons, nuts, and dried cherries. This was treatment reserved for her special pets. It was not just any visitor — duke or no — who was favored with the dried cherries. Even George in his

74

heyday never got so much as a glimpse of them. They were from her own private store. The nuts and wine and macaroons were household stock, but the cherries were kept in a tin box in Slack's own room. She must have flown up those stairs on wings of delight, for she wasn't gone a moment yet had assembled the feast from three different corners of the house.

Clavering proceeded to put on a performance that was as disgusting as anything I have witnessed in my life. "I am worried about you two ladies alone here and at the mercy of the smugglers," he said, dipping into the cherries.

"Officer Smith assures us there is not the least danger," I told him.

"Oh, poor Smith. He never catches anyone so refuses to believe the smugglers are active."

"I understand he caught a boatload about a week ago," I said.

"Caught them bringing two kegs down from Romney. Some catch! It's time I replace him."

"Have you been put in charge of customs?" I asked him.

"I have always had a hand in it, and in most local appointments," was his insolent reply. "I think I shall send two of my stout footmen down here at night to watch over the place for you." This was said to Slack, intimating no doubt to that besotted ninny that he didn't want a precious hair of her head touched.

"We have a butler and two footboys, as well as the groom. Thank you all the same," I told him.

"Still, I'll send my men down to give them a hand. Your butler is old, and your footboys and groom only boys."

"I would much prefer it if you keep your footmen at home."

Again the two exchanged that smile of toleration for the moonling, and Clavering hunched his hulking shoulders, taking another fistful of cherries. The pair then went on to a discussion for which I can find no other word than flirtation. Before I knew what was happening, Slack, usually so discreet, was telling the private details of her life, which involved in no small degree those of my own. I had the pleasure of hearing that I was not a *bad* child to mind, though always self-willed and headstrong to an extraordinary degree. I was a quick learner but would not apply myself unless goaded unmercifully.

"I don't envy you your task, ma'am," he told her, and held his glass out for her to refill to the brim. I wouldn't have been surprised in the least had she dashed to the cupboard for a larger glass. Slack's pets are force fed. It is the manner in which she shows favour.

I heard her tell him all the intimate minutiae of our lives, Mama's dwindling separation from her family, Papa's summer visits and eventual death, the advent of Mr Higgins, whom she had certainly never told me she disliked excessively. "He *drank*," she said with the strongest tone of disapproval, while zealously watching Clavering's glass to see if it would hold another drop.

All my damping remarks, glances at the clock, and comments that it was getting rather late went unheeded. Before long Mr Hemmings, my old beau, was dragged forth. There, the name is out. Edward Hemmings, from Wilton, now married to Edna Billings, who was fortunate to get him, smoked jackets and all. And may she never lay an eye on this story. Clavering nodded with polite interest and asked Slack, with never so much as a peep in my direction, why I had seen fit to decline his offer. "Just not the marrying kind, like myself," Slack said with a smirk.

"You were made for marriage; it is a crime to deprive some gentleman of your company," he contradicted baldly. Then at the end of her saga he posed the question that enshrined him as her new patron saint, Saint Clavering. "Now how does it come that such a charming lady as yourself is not married yet, Miss Slack?"

Yet! As though at fifty she is likely to make a match. And she, who has never had a beau in her entire life, simpered, "I guess I just never met the right man."

"I have no opinion of your Wiltshire gentlemen. They are singularly slow to have let you escape thus far," he said with a gallant bow and another handful of the cherries, which cleaned out her plate. "But it is early days yet for a young lady like you. You will have Miss Denver's saloon cluttered up with every Benedict in the community if I know anything."

"You will find the competition lively, Your Grace," I told him. "Would you like me to leave so that you can get right on with the offer tonight and beat the crowds to it?"

He laughed lightly and actually *winked* at Slack. "Not a bad idea," he replied. "But then I wouldn't want to deprive you of her company. You are fortunate to have found yourself such a treasure."

You may be forgiven for thinking I have overlooked some references to myself, at only twenty-five, being still eligible for marriage. None were made. Twenty-five was much too old, but fifty was next door to infancy.

Finally he arose and said, "I look forward with the greatest pleasure to seeing you both at Belview tomorrow. Are you sure you wouldn't like me to send my men, Miss Denver?"

"It's not a bad . . ." Slack began.

"Quite sure, thank you," I cut in.

"*A demain*, then," he bowed and was off, at a good pace considering the quantity of wine, cherries, and other food he had taken aboard.

"Well, he seems very nice," Slack told me with a loose-lipped grin that brought forcibly to mind my cousin George.

"You are a fool," I told her, and walked from the room before I said a good deal more which I would regret. But like any young thing with a new beau, she wished to talk about him, and came into my room before retiring.

"Did you notice, Priscilla, he didn't once mention buying Seaview tonight?"

"Even the simple can be taught if one has the patience to repeat herself often enough. Let us hope he has learned I have no intention of selling."

"Well, *I* think he is very civil."

"Do you, Slack? *I* think he is very sly. Good night." She took the hint and left.

CHAPTER
SIX

The autumn, so far from being wet and cold, was one of very good weather, better than is normally encountered on the coast, I was given to understand. The next morning was bright and bracing, not cold, but pleasantly brisk. It was ideal riding weather, and my first activity after breakfast was to go to the stable and again be hoisted on to Juliette's back. My knee had recovered from its little twist, and I had no intention of acquiring another injury, so followed Clavering's advice and walked around the garden, under the stern eye of Jemmie, the stable boy, swollen to a huge proportion by the importance of the duty fallen on his slender shoulders. "Jist straighten your shoulders a mite, miss," he would suggest, while regarding me intently. This was my worst fault, a hunching forward in fright and in readiness to grab the mane in case of trouble. It was very dull, seven times around the garden at a walk, with seven injunctions to straighten my shoulders. The walking pace increased slightly with each circuit — Juliette's idea, I must admit. She was more bored with this sluggardly performance than I. Finally I gave her a touch of my heel and she trotted. Five times around trotting (with straight shoulders) and I touched her side again, bringing her to a canter. This, I felt, would be my preferred pace. It was smoother than the trot, and fast enough to be exciting without causing the terror of a gallop, with heels flying and mud divots being thrown up behind us. Actually I was petrified of the canter, too, at this stage but felt that with time I would master it and go cantering into the village or through my aunt's park at a respectable gait. At eleven o'clock Lord Inglewood arrived for his morning's flirtation and was sent by Slack to the garden to watch me perform. I assumed that George had been dethroned with the coronation of Clavering as King Flirt.

George is almost entirely senseless, but what little he knows centers around riding and hunting. He gave me some helpful pointers. He showed me the proper manner in which to hold the reins. Why it should be required to hold them in such an unnatural manner, laced between one's fingers, I still do not know, but have observed since that it is the approved way and I was determined to do the thing properly. I found his repeated injunctions to relax difficult to achieve, but tried to relax. Juliette is sensitive, he said, could tell I was nervous, and that made her nervous. She was becoming just a trifle frolicsome to suit me, and I dismounted to go into the saloon with George. He made a few deprecatory remarks, intended, I believe, for potential compliments after I had got a better seat, that at least I didn't flop in the saddle like a sack of meal, and after I thawed out a bit, I wouldn't sit like a block of ice either. We shall see.

"What you ought to do if you mean to ride is get yourself a habit made up," Slack told me. I already knew it, of course. I had looked for a pattern in Eastbourne but not found one I liked.

"We'll go to town now and pick a pattern and some material," I said, for it was plain George had been ordered to hang about till ejected.

"It's getting close to luncheon," Slack reminded me.

"We'll have it in town. It will be a change for us," I said, and she, ever the gadabout, was not hard to convince.

George left, to have his ears singed by his mama for not accompanying us, I imagine. But at least he would have news to carry home, and that was a fraction of his duty. Slack had told him of our pending visit to Belview. I felt Lady Ing would come in person in the morning to hear all details.

I chose for my habit a rather dashing bottle green serge, and purchased a plain riding bonnet to go with the outfit. Black buttons and braid were selected and a pattern — a pleasant morning's diversion, followed by an equally pleasant luncheon at the Lighthouse Inn. There was one incident during the luncheon which displeased Slack, however, since it cast her new beau in a bad light. The servant who brought our meal was a cripple. He had a left foot that dragged behind the other. It made service slow, but one feels compassion for the disabled, of course, and Slack asked him in a kindly way just before we left what had happened to him.

"I fell into one of the Dook's mantraps," he said. "Well, I don't blame him. He was posted, but it's hard times, lady, and a man has to feed his family. He didn't prosecute," he added, perhaps to let us know he did not have a criminal record.

"Very kind of him, I'm sure!" I said, and reached into my reticule for a larger pourboire.

"So much for your Duke of Clavering," I told Slack.

"He had his signs posted," she said defensively.

"Very handy for those who can read. You are no doubt aware many of the lower classes cannot."

"That servant could. He wrote out our bill, so he can read, and knew he was taking a risk."

She was beyond reason. We stopped to chat to a few acquaintances, and decided to go to the wharf for a view of the ocean before returning home. We were still new enough to the coast that we enjoyed to admire the spectacle of the ocean from all viewpoints. It was livelier here, at the port, than at our own cove, of course. The fishing boats had gone out and were not yet due in, but other commercial vessels were to be seen, and one ship of the Royal Navy was out anchored in the harbour, looking very trim with its white ensign flapping in the breeze.

"There'll be rollicking in the streets tonight if the ship is to dock here," Slack informed me.

I spotted Officer Smith across the way, doing nothing but looking at the ocean like ourselves, so far as I could see, and no doubt making a handsome salary on our taxpayers' money for doing it.

He saw us and came toward us. "Have you had any more trouble with prowlers, Miss Denver?" he asked.

It was the first sign of interest; certainly he had not come out to us as he had said he would. "None. We have come to the conclusion it was not a prowler at all but some mechanical trouble in the chimney."

"Very likely," he agreed at once, always eager to absolve the smugglers of any blame for anything. I began to wonder whether he wasn't in sympathy with them, but his next speech undeceived me.

He resumed glancing out to sea. There were several vessels in sight, but I felt he was looking at one in particular. It looked like a fishing boat to me, what the local people call a yawl, I believe. It has two masts and was a fair-sized thing. I have to this day difficulty distinguishing a boat from a ship. As surely as I use one term, my companion uses the other, placing just enough emphasis on the word to let me know I am in error. The difference seems to have to do with size — at some point a boat becomes a ship, but the turning point I have not yet determined. The same thing plagues me with ponies and horses.

"There's the *Nancy-Jane* dancing around, up to no good," Smith told me.

"You think it's a smuggler's boat?" I asked, following the line of his eyes.

"It's *his* ship," Smith said, pointing to a great hulk of a man ten or twelve yards away. *Ship* — wrong again. The lounging man wore a black toque, from which reddish hair stuck out, a black sweater and a pair of trousers that were dirt coloured and might possibly once have been fawn. "I *know* it's used for smuggling."

"Why don't you arrest him?" I asked.

"He isn't carrying a load. I've been out."

"You have actually to catch him with the brandy aboard, do you?" I asked.

"Oh, yes. We need our evidence," he replied, shocked at my question. "He is waiting for a good day to slip across the Channel."

"You mentioned the other day you thought there was just the one smuggler here now. Is this the man?"

"That's him. Louie FitzHugh. Lazy Louie they call him, and a less apt name would be hard to imagine. He's an eel is what he is."

I glanced toward him, and Lazy Louie seemed the more appropriate term. He stood in a lounging position doing absolutely nothing. I recognized the name as the same one Mr McMaster had mentioned.

"He was caught bribing revenue officers, was he not?"

"It was suspected. They couldn't prove anything. They laid off the officers and the criminal went scot free. There's justice for you."

"If the officers were taking bribes, they, too, were criminals, criminals paid out of the public purse."

"Yes, *if* they were taking bribes. If the officers were guilty, then Louie FitzHugh is more guilty, but he goes on breaking the law, unmolested."

"It is your duty to molest him, officer," I pointed out.

"Only if he brings it in within the bounds of my jurisdiction. I think he must bring it in up the Romney coast. He is clean by the time he comes here, but you can smell it yards away, the brandy, on *Nancy-Jane*. The smell lingers, you know, there is no hiding it; but every time I board he's clean. I'd like to know where he puts it ashore. Up Romney way they say he doesn't come in there, but he must. He certainly doesn't land it at Clavering's shore. The Duke has his own patrol, and Lazy Louie is his special target. I work closely with Clavering. We are both determined to get him. Still, there's no point watching him today. *Nancy-Jane* has no cargo but a half-load of fish, and they're two days old or I miss my bet. Taken aboard to kill the smell of brandy. There, his horse is being brought to him now. Has a groom, like a gentleman, to look after his mount, and what a fine animal it is. I wish I had one half as good."

A sleek, black animal was being led forth by a boy who was no worse groomed than his master. Rather better, in fact. Lazy Louie took the reins and mounted with a graceful, effortless movement that I envied. It was something achieved only by men, though. In the same easy way did Clavering stride his mount. Horse and rider turned and galloped off into town without so much as a glance at Officer Smith. This was the height of arrogance — not to even glance at your enemy. Really, there was a touch of Clavering's arrogance in the man, as well as his equestrian ability.

"The fellow has a house, too. Lives in altogether too high a style for a fisherman that is not at market two days a week, nor one half the time. He's a smuggler, not a doubt of it, and one day I'll catch him," Officer Smith promised. The grim set of his lips made me think he had been saying the same thing for some time. Maybe it was time Clavering did replace this ineffectual recipient of taxpayers' money.

Slack began twitching at my arm, as though she hadn't a tongue in her head, and I was made to realize it was time to go home. I spoke to her regarding Clavering and his mantraps on the way home, but not a word against him would she utter. When she likes someone, she is as faithful as a dog. She pointed out that he was within his legal rights to protect his valuable Roman ruins, and no regard for *moral* rights would turn her from her decision. He wasn't even allowed to have a flaw, let alone a fault.

"I doubt that poor servant at the inn, with likely a dozen children to feed, was after his precious Roman ruins. A hare or a pheasant was all he wanted, and he is to spend the rest of his life a cripple because Clavering likes his privacy. I daresay he has maimed half the town. There is the helper in the butcher's shop who is lame, too."

"He has a club foot. He was born crippled, and the servant at the inn *shouldn't* have a dozen children if he can't afford to feed them without stealing."

"Yes, Professor Malthus. Are we going to have a dissertation now on the necessity for moral restraint of the passion between the sexes? You go ahead and set out your shingle as an economist, and I shall employ my time more usefully by telling the Duke of Clavering what I think of his mantraps."

To give him a piece of my mind, I put on my yellow lutestring gown, and rather wished it were dinner we were going to, so that I might wear the dashing green silk instead. No doubt the dinner party he had been entertaining before was composed of ladies gowned in the highest kick of fashion, and there was no reason Slack and I should appear as utter dowds before him. Slack's only concession to the occasion was a negative one, namely bringing forth her old mustard-coloured netted shawl, which she *still*, after five years, refers to her as her "good" shawl. Really, he would take us for a pair of quizzes. With some difficulty, I got her to borrow my more elegant white cashmere before I recalled that I ought to take it myself. However, my gown had long sleeves, and Belview might be less windy than Seaview — Hillcrest — I must really get busy and find a new name.

It was this subject that made up our conversation en route to Belview. Slack, in the throes of her passion for the Duke, made not a single contribution. Seaview was a perfect name. Did we not have a view of the sea? "Yes, and a view of Clavering's spinney and the road as well, but we don't call it Spinneyview, or Roadview." My suggestion of Seacrest, combining her favourite and mine, was talked down as absurd, since the sea did not crest at our front door. "Denver Manor, then," I essayed. Slack pointed out, quite properly, that as I had not lands, let alone lands from which I extracted fees, the name was ineligible. There was one lone willow tree drooping over the home garden and quite ruining the produce of half that spot, and I thought I might call it

Willow Hall, but no conclusion was reached when we turned up the tree-lined road that led to Belview.

We both stopped discussing names and goggled about without reserve. The road wound about this way and that like a snake, giving various vistas of rolling lawns, groups of trees, bushes, and once a gaggle of geese. At length it straightened to a broad curve, and Belview came into sight. It was enormous. The size of it was quite staggering. It stretched to left and right of an impressive recessed doorway and rose three stories high. The only feature in common with Seaview (or whatever the place should properly be called) was the lancet windows, and it was only on the ground floor that Belview had such windows. Perhaps other stories had been added later. The windows above were not so flamingly Gothic, with ornaments, but only pointed at the top for purposes of cohesion of design, I surmised. In fact, the place was an eclectic blend of Gothic and fortress, giving strangely the effect of a church transformed into a garrison, but it was cleverly done, so that the turrets on either end of the facade and the crenellated line of roof between did not look absurd at all. In such a large piece of architecture there was room for a variety of styles. I thought I had seen bartizans from the road, but they were not visible from the front. We looked our fill of the front, then went up the half dozen stairs to the doorway. Looking behind us, Belview, at least, we saw to be well named. The view was *très belle* indeed. On the door there was a brass knocker in the shape of an anchor, in deference to our location by the sea. It was not quite so large as a real anchor, but heavy enough that I felt the weight when I lifted it.

It took no more than one knock to bring the butler, and as we were shown in, our eyes were again busy to take in the many glories of Belview. A veritable ocean of shiny oaken floors stretched into the distance before us, and to the left an ornately carved grand staircase with shallow, broad steps led upstairs, the stairway wall hung with painted faces, ancestors of the Duke. They were all as ugly as he, dark, and saturnine, even the women.

As I peered up at these framed faces, the flesh-and-blood Clavering descended, running lightly in a manner that was at odds with all the solemn formality of the house. He smiled faintly at me, reserving his better expression for his lady friend.

"How kind of you to come," he said to her.

While she gushed out her delight at being here, I took another look around. No statues in niches, in fact, no niches. The walls were straight, covered with yellow silk, with a gilt-edged mirror hanging over a carved table where flowers in a real tub made of brass nodded at themselves in the mirror. But then the hallway was so immense that anything less than a tub would have been lost. How odd it was to think of one man living all alone in this museum of a home, with his fifty bedrooms.

We were shown into a room that bore not one single sign of a resemblance to Seaview (you know where I mean) except for the pointed windows along the front wall, and it was supposedly its resemblance to our own home that had brought us here. Someone in that house was fond of yellow. As in the hall with its yellow walls, there was a quantity of yellow in this room. The draperies were gold, and there were golden and green sofas and chairs spaced around the room between tables and windows. It was all very elegant, too much so for my taste, with fine Persian carpets whose price I was familiar with from looking for replacements at home. A welter of priceless bibelots, porcelain, jade, and faience, littered the surfaces of the furniture. Lady Inglewood would have been *aux anges*; she liked a room to look cluttered. For myself, I like things neat and tidy. I took pains that not a jot of admiration escape my eyes, but after I had been seated a few minutes, I discovered that a feeling of happy peace came over me. The yellow was well chosen; it brought sunshine into the room, and there was some tranquility transferred by the order of the place, the two fireplaces ranged along the outer wall, not marble but again carved in oak. There was a good deal of carving throughout the place.

Slack had been dumping the butter boat on him in praise of every chair and footstool in the room. "Very pleasant," I complimented him, so as not to appear surly.

"Thank you," he replied punctiliously. "A pity you could not have had a ride today, Miss Denver. The weather hasn't turned bad yet."

"I did ride," I said, before I recalled the full day I had outlined to him.

"For an hour before we went calling," Slack threw in, rather deftly, I must confess.

90

He was out to win us and did not suggest by a single gesture that he didn't believe it. "You are wise to take every opportunity before the gales arrive," was all he said.

"Well, would you like your tea now or later? You were going to have a look around the house."

"I'm not at all hungry yet," Slack said, though he had actually put the question to me, but I, too was more curious than hungry, and the house was to be seen first.

"This is the Marine Saloon," he said, taking us to the hall and off to the right. We entered a large, well-lit room, whose only claim to being a Marine Room was two huge glass-fronted cabinets full of shells and a clutch of dull marinescapes hung on the walls. Other than that, it was another sitting-room, done in depressing shades of blue and green, with sea-green window hangings.

"We have done it in sea shades," he said, and walked to one of the cabinets. There were all kinds of shells, some great things as big as a man's head in conch and other convoluted shapes, as well as one flatter one of the oyster shell shape that was between twelve and eighteen inches across, and had a whole shelf to itself. From these giant sizes they ranged down to some no bigger than my thumb. I mentioned that I had never seen such interesting variety on our beach, and learned that an ancestor had collected these specimens from all over the world. The acquisitive streak was deep-rooted in the family, as was the labelling streak. Each shell had its own card. I found my interest in shells to be not so great as either Clavering's or Slack's. For an interminable length of time she lifted them up one by one, marvelling that it had come from Jamaica or Brazil, or whatever the card might say. More marvelous to me was that anyone could have been bothered either going or sending around the globe for such worthless objects, and then to set them up as an ornamental feature.

Slack's questions all answered, we went into a pokey little study, a dark and uninviting chamber. "This is the room that most closely resembles Seaview," he told us. It was not so very unlike my largest saloon, but still it was an unhappy comparison, his worst and my best. There was the same panelling high up on the walls, roughly the same dimensions, though it looked smaller after his own huge saloons, and was not so well windowed. My new rose draperies, too, made my own saloon appear more elegant than this one we stood in. Our attention was called to some carving by someone named Grinling Gibbons, who had also done the carving at Seaview, not for my house actually. It had originally decorated a bedchamber at Belview and been physically prised from there to decorate my saloon. A singularly futile arrangement, in my view, but I assume Miss Tilbridge had admired Grinling Gibbons a good deal more than I did myself.

"But it is really my collection I want you to see," he said, when we had looked our fill at the study.

"*Another* collection?" I asked, hoping to convey the idea I did not approve of all this amassing of possessions. "My, you will have to begin collecting more houses to store so much treasure."

I could see the muscle in his jaw work with the effort of being civil at this taunt, but when he spoke he maintained his calm. "My Roman things. I keep them in the library, for lack of a better spot."

They made a great mess of his library. The room would have been very well if not littered with broken bits of rubbish. Smashed heads of statues, some minus a nose, some with a whole chin knocked off, legs, feet, arms, and hands were spread over tables much too good for this rough usage. What anyone could want with this marble anatomy passed imagining. Bits and pieces other than human were there, too, pridefully displayed as though they were *objects d'art*. There were pots and jugs with and without handles and in various states of disrepair. One very large and ugly piece sat alone in state on a pedestal that would more properly have held an unbroken piece of statuary. This piece was a head, even dirty and encrusted with moss — of an old soldier, I thought.

"I believe this is a head of Mithras," he said, looking at us for praise.

"Very handsome," Slack humoured him. "Who was Mithras?"

"A Persian sun god."

"I thought it was Roman — *things* you collected?" I hardly knew what word to apply to his debris.

"He was discovered in Persia by the legionnaries and became the soldiers' deity. He came right along to Britain with them."

"Imagine that; it came all the way from Persia!" Slack said, craning her neck the better to view the oddity.

"No, no, it was rather the idea they brought with them. This was carved in Britain — it is native stone," he said, offended.

"I didn't think anyone would have bothered carrying it all the way from Persia," I said. Again the jaws twitched, and again he contained his spleen.

The only piece in the entire collection that had the least approval from me was a brass statue of a young girl. Slack cast only a cursory glance at it, since the young girl was undraped. "Stark naked", she later described it to me, shocked. But it was neither chipped nor broken nor bent, and it was better than most of his treasures in my estimation.

"I have much more in the attics," he told us. I hurriedly proclaimed there was not the least necessity to have them brought down. He spoke for some time of coins and swords and "artifacts," which appeared to be everyday carpentry tools, surgical instruments, and farming implements, of which a nearly exact replica could be bought today in any shop.

"They really ought to be available for the public to see," he finished up his lecture.

I was quite simply amazed that he would speak of sharing his things with anyone, let alone the unwashed public. Crowds of curious gawkers tramping through Belview could not be what he had in mind. "How would you do it?" I asked. "You wouldn't want anyone here."

94

"Well, I wouldn't want *everyone* here, in my home," he said, with just a glint of understanding, I think. "In fact, I have a confession to make. Help me, Miss Slack."

Slack would gladly have helped him chop off a head, such a state of infatuation had she achieved, but her blank stare told me that she was not in league with him on this mysterious matter, at least.

"The fact is, I hope to set up a small museum," he said, in the tone of an announcement. "Eastbourne has one, and Pevensey could do with one, too. It is really a shame that so few know about or *care* about our Roman heritage."

"This is a strange thing to feel you must *confess*," I told him. "There can be no harm in opening a museum."

"Ah, but the museum I have in mind is Seaview. It is particularly appropriate . . ."

"It happens to be occupied!" I pointed out sharply. "And its appropriateness I must say escapes me, that being the case, unless you feel Miss Slack and I are ancient enough to be displayed as antiques."

"Shall we go back to the Yellow Saloon and sit down?" he suggested in an attempt to turn aside my wrath. He thought I would be too civil to argue over the teacups, a view in which he was mistaken.

He raised an eyebrow at a servant who passed us in the hall, which was a command to bring tea. A silver tray that required a very stout man to carry it was soon placed on the tea table.

"Would you be kind enough to pour, Miss Denver?" he asked. I lifted, with some trouble, the large silver pot and poured into fine Wedgwood cups. Dainty sandwiches had been made, and they were delicious. A tempting variety of sweets were also laid out on a tiered dish. It was an excellent tea.

I was not turned from my track by it, however. "You were saying you may consider *my* home particularly suitable for your museum. Would you be kind enough to explain that rather strange statement, Your Grace?"

"Oh, dear!" he said, and set down his cup. It sounded an absurdly mild phrase to issue from that swarthy face. "I always feel, you know, when young ladies go on calling me 'Your Grace' that I have offended them. But there is justice in selecting Seaview as the site of the museum. I do not consider it peculiarly my own, the museum. I intend endowing it, but giving it to the town."

"I don't know about justice, but there is surely some injustice in cashiering a private dwelling for such a purpose."

"No injustice is intended. You recall we spoke of thirty-five hundred pounds."

"No, Your Grace, I recall *you* spoke of thirty-five hundred pounds. I recall as well you had an invalid aunt on whose behalf you sought the place. Tell me, has there been a sudden death in your family, or has she recovered from her serious lung trouble without benefit of our local gales?"

"I had hoped to appeal to your tender compassion for an elderly invalid. Finding such an emotion lacking,

96

I revert to business instead. There is an invalid aunt, incidentally. I had thought I might put my Aunt Eileen there till I had the museum plans settled, hoping a year by the sea might do her good. But you give me no opportunity to explain my mentioning justice. Seaview is built on the remains of a Roman fort, of course . . ."

"A Roman fort? I heard nothing of that!" I exclaimed.

"Did you not? But surely you mentioned to me having been in the cellars the other day. You must have seen the stone wall."

"Stone wall? Certainly I saw stone walls, one vastly superior to the others . . ."

"The wall below the rattling grate is the remains of one of the old Roman forts. I blush to confess my great-grandfather had the unwisdom to build over it. The desecration that has been done to the Roman ruins is really appalling. The fort was one of the chain that formed the fortification known as the Forts of the Saxon Shore. From Richborough to Portsmouth, to guard against invasion. Porchester Castle is another of them. They were right on the shore in those days, but the sea has receded, and some of them are quite far inland now. This one is closer to the sea than most."

"I noticed that wall was finer than the others. But you mean it is actually surviving from the Roman period? How old would it be?"

"The Saxon pirates were in the Channel around A.D. 280. It would be more than fifteen hundred years old."

"Just to think!" I said, becoming excited now. "And it looks as good as new."

"Better than the stonework done today. Well, their roads still survive, and they are some of our better roads, too, straight and smooth-surfaced. They built them to last — a bed of gravel, then flint laid in cement. We have had nothing to approach them till Telford and Macadam came along just recently."

"It is only because of that wall in the basement you think my house would be suitable?"

"I said poetic justice. My family destroyed one of the old Saxon Forts. I would like to do something to repay our debt to historians and collect in one spot such material as I can find relating to the period. Why, at Seaview even the cellars would be of interest, you see."

"Surely the city itself would be a better location — more easily accessible to everyone. Seaview is a long walk from Pevensey, and not everyone has a horse or carriage. Then, too," I added with a significant voice, "the roads are flooded every spring?"

"Not every spring," he admitted sheepishly.

"No, not since the last century, according to Lady Inglewood. But my objection still stands, and I think it is a valid one. The city itself would be the better location."

"The old Roman fort was actually standing there, you know. It would give a great sense of being there, to realize that where you stood looking at the artifacts Roman soldiers actually once looked out at the invaders."

"I see your point. A great sense of immediacy would be gained," Slack took it up, nodding her head at his every word. It infuriated me to see her make up to him so.

"You speak of fifteen hundred years ago or more, Your Grace. Nineteen years will be as a drop in the bucket when you are speaking of millenia. In nineteen years you can set up your museum. Meanwhile, I see no reason why I should give up my home for your hobby."

"To benefit the community," he said simply.

"I doubt the community at large has much interest in Roman remains. I suggest if you feel this wild passion in benefiting the community, you rid your lands of mantraps before you maim anyone else."

"Ah, you have met Leo Milkin."

"I heard from the servant at the Lighthouse what happened to him. Kind of you not to prosecute!"

"That's Milkin."

"I wasn't sure he wasn't another of your victims."

"There has been only one victim."

"So far! One is one too many — to see that poor man crippled for life because you . . ."

"He fell into the . . ." he began suddenly, then stopped as suddenly, as if he disliked to do so, as if he wanted to say more, give some excuse for his behavior.

I had determined to bring the matter to Clavering's attention and I had done it. It pretty effectually ruined the tea party, and I saw Slack was unhappy with me, but I was glad I had done it nevertheless. I would have felt morally negligent had I not.

"You are not at all interested in my project then?" he asked stiffly.

"It sounds an excellent project, but I suggest you find yourself another location."

"I *mean*, as I think you realize, you will not sell Seaview to me?"

"Prove to me you really care about benefiting the community," I suggested. "Remove the mantraps, and we'll discuss the matter."

"Impossible!" he said, without even giving it a moment's thought.

One word revealed him for the hypocrite he was — the arrogant, overbearing, selfish hypocrite. He no more cared for truly benefiting the people than I cared for his old museum. He had a hobby that amused him for the present while. The choice of Seaview as its location told me it was for his personal pleasure. No thought to the convenience of the visitors occurred to him.

"Also impossible for me to sell my house, which, incidentally, I have called Willow Hall," I said, and arose with a commanding look at Slack to accompany me. She said not a word in the hero's defence, but looked disappointed in him. I had some hopes this incident would return her to her usual good sense.

"That is absurd! It is not a hall, and there isn't a willow anywhere near it!" he answered angrily, but, of course, it wasn't the new name that angered him so much as my daring not to do as he wished.

"You are mistaken. There is a beautiful willow tree in the back garden, and if I want to call it a hall, I will."

He glared, the jaw working, and I went on politely. "Thank you for the tea, Your Grace, and the tour. Both very enjoyable. Do feel free to call on us at Willow Hall any time you are passing by." This was pure irony, and of no very high calibre either, I realize, but he wasn't the only one who was angry. Naturally he would not call again.

"You're making a mistake, Miss Denver," he said in a cold, hard voice that sounded strangely like a threat.

"Do you think so? Who knows, you may tire of collecting bits of broken old rubbish soon and will be happy I saved you the expense of buying them a home," I answered in a honeyed voice.

"Don't say I didn't warn you," he replied, then turned us over to the butler for showing out. While we were still in the hallway he was going up the stairs, showing us his back in a very underbred way. Slack didn't say a word in his defence as I reviled him scathingly all the way home. As we dismounted she even went so far as to say, "I am disappointed in him."

"I'm not. It is no more than I expected from him."

CHAPTER
SEVEN

That night the grate took to jumping as it had not jumped before. I do not suggest it was in any way connected with Clavering's veiled threat, except that the one followed the other. *Post hoc, ergo propter hoc.* Papa often pointed out to me the flaw in this sort of reasoning. Because a black cat crosses your path and you then break your leg is not to say the cat brought your misfortune to you, but it seems to me there is a cause-and-effect relationship as often as not in our affairs. In any case, he warned me I would be sorry, and then it happened. It did not just bump once as on the other occasions. It shook for a full minute, as though a giant hand were shaking the very wall. Then it stopped till we caught our breath, then it started again, four times in all, and quite frankly it was terrifying. Well, you can imagine how you would feel if it were to happen to you.

Slack and I stared at each other mutely. What was there to say? I called Wilkins, the butler, and he looked at it in alarm. I got him to accompany me to the cellar with lights, but there was nothing new to be seen. Slack remained in the saloon to listen for voices, but she heard none. By the time we got upstairs, Wilkins and I, it had stopped. I sent the two footboys out to look around for poachers, but they reported there was no one outside. It was a formality only. Poachers bent on concealment would never have made such a din. After the noise stopped and Wilkins left, I put my idea to Slack.

"I think Clavering had something to do with it," I told her, reminding her of the threat.

He was in bad enough aroma with her that she was willing to give the idea space in her head, but neither of us could think of any means in which he could have accomplished it, and it remained a complete mystery. Furthermore, it happened again the next morning at half past ten. Giving the thing the importance of a fatal shot, we noted the time. On that occasion we were both seated by the grate. It was another dismal, rainy day. It was Sunday, but due to the weather we had stayed home from church. We had lit a small fire, for cheer rather than warmth. The grate heaved harder than before. I was half afraid the stones would topple from the wall and land in the middle of the floor. It shook for a minute and a half by the clock, then stopped, and I am willing to swear on a Bible that I heard the sound of echoing laughter coming from the chimney.

I went as close as I could get to the flue, (with a fire burning it was not very close, of course) and called, "Who's there? Stop it at once! Do you hear?" It shook harder than ever, and I jumped back, frightened half out of my wits.

"It's a ghost! It is!" Slack told me, and blessed herself.

"A ducal ghost," I replied angrily. *Don't say I didn't warn you.* "I'll go to Pevensey tomorrow and get a builder to come out and look at the house," I said. Till then, I could think of nothing to do.

Fortunately the shaking and the laughter stopped then, but to look at the grate, to enter the room even, was becoming an ordeal. I could not ride Juliette due to the weather. In the afternoon the rain abated but did not stop entirely. Lady Inglewood and George came to call and were treated not only to a telling of our trip to Belview but to an account of the stunts of the grate as well. There is surely no exercise in the world so depressing, so exasperating, so absolutely demoralizing as trying to make sane, sensible people believe the unbelievable. If I ever see a ghost, I won't tell a soul. I shall keep it to myself, for I wouldn't endure the superior smiles of my aunt or people like her again for any reason. Even with Slack there as my witness, to imitate for them the hollow laughter we had heard, Lady Ing didn't believe it. Wilkins added his version, but still disbelief was writ on her face. George, I think, was more believing. His mother spoke reassuring words of winds and draughts and loose bricks. I could have throttled her.

She did not miss the opportunity of putting George forward as our protector. The poor man was sent scurrying from cellar to attic, but I knew he would find nothing, which is exactly what he found. I told Aunt Ethelberta that Clavering meant to set up a museum, which interested her very little. She said he had been riding this hobbyhorse forever but never did any more than talk about it. She was more curious to hear what we had to eat, and whether anyone else besides ourselves had been there. She was put out she had not been asked, too, but absolved him of insult by deciding he was angry with her for not offering Seaview to him first.

The only other item of interest that passed during the visit was for me to invite them for dinner the next week for Slack's fifty-first birthday. My aunt and George would come to dine with us. I toyed with the idea of making it a larger party. I was rather eager to toss a real party, but Slack said grumpily it was little enough to celebrate, getting another year older, and she wanted no large party. It was true it was I who wanted a bigger do, so I would hold it later and not pretend it was in Slack's honour.

We passed an utterly dreary day, the only thing of the least use that was accomplished was the beginning of my riding habit, and that I suppose ought not really to have been commenced on the Sabbath. We got it cut out. Several times during the evening Slack mentioned wishing we had something to read in the house, for with autumn coming on there would be many a long evening such as this one. We found a pile of old magazines, some of them not completely ancient, in the parson's bench by the fireplace, but it became clear eventually that what Slack really wanted to read was books on Roman ruins in England. I leave it to you to conclude why this dull subject should interest her. I had thought she was over her infatuation for Clavering upon discovering him to be incurably selfish and cruel, but apparently not.

By the next morning the rain had stopped, but it was by no means a pleasant day. The sky was the colour of Slack's oldest shawl. I don't know whether it is grey or purple, but a very dull, ominous colour. We went to Pevensey to ask the builder to come and look over the chimney, but he was very busy and couldn't come for a few days. At Slack's insistence we also made a stop at the circulating library. They had exactly one book on Roman ruins, and it was a detailed description with drawings of the baths at Bath. Undaunted, she took it out, but I doubted she would get far in her courting of Clavering with it and suggested that if she was to set up as an expert on the ruins in Sussex, she would do better to order herself some more useful reference books. She baulked at the price, but I reminded her that her birthday was approaching, and they would be my gift. What she *needed*, of course, was a new shawl, but then a birthday is no time to be giving a person a necessity. A gift ought to be a luxury, or it is not a real gift. I had a more luxurious luxury picked out for her, as well; Slack will not accept a penny more than she was paid when my parents were alive, despite my greatly enlarged fortune, and I had to use such ruses as this to reward her a little more adequately.

We did not eat at the inn but brought home our dinner fresh from the fishermen at the wharf. I observed the "ship" *Nancy-Jane* was still dancing in the harbour but saw neither Lazy Louis nor lazy Officer Smith. The sullen skies had toned down to pearl grey by afternoon, and I had a little lesson on Juliette before going in to stitch up my new green riding habit. I half thought, to be truthful, that Slack would already have begun doing this for me, but I found her with her head in the book about Bath. She is not paid to be my seamstress but usually helps me out in my sewing, and in this case where there was some urgency in finishing my habit I would have welcomed her assistance.

"This is very interesting, Priscilla," she told me. "'Aquae Sulis,' Bath used to be called. I know the Aquae means waters, and I expect the Sulis might refer to the sulphur. It was dedicated to Minerva. I didn't know that, did you?"

"No, Slack, and have hobbled along very well all these years without knowing it, too. I think I'll begin working on my riding habit."

"The baths were used for medicinal purposes, of course. The water came out of the springs at one hundred and twenty degrees. Fancy that."

"There must have been some parboiled Romans at Aquae Sulis, I fancy. Well, I think I'll start the jacket first," I said and picked up a sleeve, thinking she would offer to help me.

"The baths at Aquae Sulis are quite different from the baths they built elsewhere — larger and more impressive altogether. They actually had swimming baths there, Priscilla. Only think, the engineering feat. They still exist, just like our wall, one rectangular, the largest, with a lead floor, and two circular baths. I can hardly credit that we *lived* in Wiltshire for twenty-four years and never had the sense to go to Bath to see these Roman ruins."

"We had neither of us succumbed to gout or rheumatism or to the Duke of Clavering at the time," I told her, a little sharply. She chose to ignore it.

"There is a museum there, too. How I should love to see it! You really must have a look at this book, Priscilla. I never read anything so interesting. They found many coins and even precious stones thrown in the springhead, and it is believed they were thrown in as offerings to the gods. To Minerva, I suppose, since it was dedicated to her. Isn't it odd how we go about our lives without ever giving a thought to the past?"

"Some of us are becoming so immersed in it we never give a thought to the present. May I disturb your research to ask you for those venerable artifacts, the scissors?"

She felt about for them and passed them over without ever taking her eyes from the book. I worked alone on my riding habit till dinner. Slack read aloud oftener than was pleasant, about chalybeate springs and other things that meant no more to me than they did to her. She discussed strange circles of stones found standing not far from Bath, apparently the remains of some temple, and hinted at least seven times that she would certainly like to go to Aquae Sulis for a visit. In a fit of pique, I suggested she move there, for it seemed her mind was rotting and the chalybeate waters might restore it. At this she finally took the hint and set the book aside, but it was time for dinner by then, and so I got no help in my sewing.

We had not seen either of the Inglewoods all day, and I was fairly sure George would come over in the evening. He did not, nor did anyone call. It was a long, dull evening. The next few days passed in much this same way. I, working alone at my riding habit, spent the better part of the week finishing it, for though I am not a despicable needlewoman, I had considerable trouble fitting the jacket all alone and had to rip it out twice. Slack had become a confirmed amateur historian, an instant expert on the subject of Aquae Sulis. I rode Juliette on the good days, and though I did not achieve Slack's degree of competence with Bath, I got over my worst nervousness and could canter around the garden without mortal terror. The Inglewoods came a few times, and one day we took tea with them. Slack was given no opportunity to show off her newly acquired knowledge. Clavering stayed away. We met him once in the village, where we had gone to see if by chance the circulating library had had another book on Roman ruins returned during our absence, but it hadn't.

His Grace was kind enough to lift his hat and say, "How do you do?" in arctic accents. I believe Slack addressed a few remarks to him, but as Lazy Louie came trotting down the road on his big black stallion at that same time, my interest was turned to him. I wondered if Clavering, his sworn enemy, would say anything to him, issue any warning about taking *Nancy-Jane* out. He looked up as Lazy Louie rode by. They exchanged a meaningful look but did not speak. Glancing from one face to the other, I was struck by some little similarity between them — a way of holding the head it was, a stiff, arrogant, proud posture. Why a smuggler should hold his head so high I could not imagine, but I assumed his fine mount and fine home in town had given him ideas above his station.

We were no sooner home than Slack stuck her nose in her book again, and I was left alone with my riding habit, the neck of which I was having considerable trouble with. No number of hints had the least effect on my companion, and in a fit of pique I set it aside. I would go to the attic and rout amongst the discarded lumber there for retrievable objects. This was one part of my new home that had not been thoroughly gone over, and I harboured the foolish hope that I would uncover some rare piece of furniture or bibelot cast aside by one without my discerning eye. About the only thing worth carrying downstairs was a firescreen, in better shape than the one we had thrown out, and as it seemed our new one would never be completed, mentally tagged it for rescue. For the rest, there was nothing worth having carried up so many flights of stairs. It would make good burning in the grate, however. Before descending, I went to the window and surveyed the countryside. From this high vantage point I had a view of more of Belview than the tops of its towers, a better view than was allowed from the road. Seeing it from the east side rather than from the front, I noticed the number and size of the outbuildings, large stables, barns, ice house, and assorted little buildings whose function I could only imagine. My position gave a good view of the meadow, too, and I had my first glimpse of the ruined chapel of which I had heard so much. It was well and truly ruined; there was not a wall standing higher than a yard off the ground. No interesting spaces to show where the windows had been, or even the style of it. I looked, trying to gauge the distance from the spinney's end to the chapel, to see if I could have a better view of the chapel from there, and as I looked, I noticed some movement.

There were two figures, and I was not so far away that I mistook them for anything but human figures. Two men were walking hastily and stealthily through the meadows, in the direction of the chapel. The hair on my scalp prickled, to think of the danger they were in. This was what I had dreaded, that some poor illiterate souls would wander unsuspectingly into that trap-infested area, to have their legs mangled and go limping through the rest of their lives, like the man at the inn. The local people all knew about the traps, so these must be strangers to the area. They should be warned, but how to get to them without falling into the traps myself? I at least knew the traps were there. I must risk it, and walk very carefully. I ran, rather than walked, and decided to make the trip on Juliette to save time. I let her out to a canter as we went through the spinney, not slowing the pace till we came to the meadow's edge. The grass was long at the summer's end. Such a waste, no cattle grazing here, nor the hay even mown, and there were some considerable number of acres. So ideal, of course, for concealing the treacherous traps. Losing a foot was not the worst that could happen here. If one were left undiscovered, he could lose his life. I gazed beyond, searching for the men, and saw nothing. I had to take myself by the scruff of the neck and make myself advance for I was quite weak with fright.

At a careful walk, straining my eyes forward at every step, we advanced, Juliette and I, till we were within shouting distance of where I had seen the men. Then I began shouting and continued to do so till I got right up to the chapel, but there was no answering call, nor even a sign of the men. They had vanished. There was one mound of rock higher than the others, and I dismounted to clamber up on it for a better view, all in vain. The men were not to be seen. The thing was impossible, but it had happened. They couldn't *both* be dead in a trap so soon. I looked beyond the ruins, but the tall grass was undisturbed. Behind me was my own path and theirs, several yards away, highly visible as a parting in the grass. Both trails stopped at the ruins.

This was my first opportunity to view the remains of the chapel, and I was highly curious to do so, but becoming more frightened than curious. The men could be crouching behind any pile of rocks, hiding with the intention of attacking me. I did no more than glance at a smallish excavation, a family chapel, not a church, with a few stones still remaining. Hardly sufficient to worry about anyone stealing, for they would not get the reconstructed temple two feet off the ground. My mind full of unanswered questions, I returned home through the same depression in the grass through which I had come, knowing it to be free of danger.

I now had another mystery to go along with my clanking grate, and as if to increase my apprehension, that object took to rattling again on Thursday. It was Slack who lifted her head from her book long enough to come up with a sort of an idea, one culled from her new interest, of course. "I wonder if it would be possible we are sitting on buried treasure," she said. "It would account for Clavering's not wanting anyone wandering about his lands; and if he doesn't know exactly where it's buried, it would account as well for his wanting to get Seaview back so that he could search for it here."

"We are on the coast — pirate's treasure! Some of Captain Morgan's loot from Cuba or Panama," I said, taking it up the more eagerly to keep Slack's interest from Bath.

"I was thinking more of some Clavering treasure, buried at one time or another due to some of the wars, the civil war or such."

"Or concealed in the house itself! That would account for his being willing to pay thirty-five hundred pounds for the house. Slack, shall we have a house hunt?"

"You're talking of ripping up floors and tearing out panelling, are you?" she asked, a trifle sarcastically, I believe. "It wouldn't be hidden under the rug, or anything of that sort."

"I have a much better idea. I'll tear my house apart, stone from stone, at the end of nineteen years, and if there is any treasure hidden, we shall get it then."

"Yes, an excellent idea," she said, but I had already lost her to antiquity. Her voice had that vague quality with which she told me linen would be fine for lunch, or yes, a cabbage would make a marvellous shawl. This was the sort of conversation we had recently. She was off in another world, and to all intents and purposes I talked to myself.

On Friday morning, I found a more conversable person. Mr Pickering, the builder, came from Pevensey to investigate the phenomenon of the noisy grate.

He was a plain, no-nonsense sort of a man, and I was curious to see what he would make of it. He began his examination in the saloon, at the grate itself. He had a little rubber-tipped hammer with which he tapped the stones, the oaken shelf, the hearth floor, and chimney lining. He also had a little apparatus called a level, a metal frame with a glass tube inserted horizontally, holding some liquid with an air bubble in it. This was placed in various spots to see if the house was out of kilter, built on a slant. It was not. The bubble of air settled comfortably in the centre of the tube, and I was informed my house was "straight" or "flat." Next a measuring tape came out of his toolbox, and he measured carefully, muttering to himself the while.

"You've got yourself a mighty fine fireplace, ma'am. Your trouble ain't here. I'll just throw a ladder up to your roof and have a gander of your chimney." This was done almost with the ease of expressing the intention. He was up there for the better part of half an hour, and I was soon informed that I had a mighty fine chimney and roof, too. All nice and flat, and with no loose

114

masonry. He mentioned the possibility of a squirrel down the chimney, or a bird, but as the rattling went on during progressive days, including several in which a fire burned, I could not think a well-baked squirrel would be so rambunctious. The sounds were more in keeping with an elephant.

Next it was the basement, which was also proclaimed to be mighty fine. This was the last hope, and I went to the basement with Mr Pickering. The Roman wall he did not recognize as Roman but did recognize as being mighty fine. I told him its origin, and he was interested. "Seaview (I used the name he would recognize) is built over an old Roman fort you know," I told him. "The Duke of Clavering's ancestors were so ill-judged as to build over it."

"No," he said, shaking his head firmly.

I looked at him in surprise, pointing to the Roman wall. "The Duke himself told me," I said.

"He's wrong," the man said simply. I don't know why it should be, but the remark filled me with joy. How happy I was to hear that Clavering was wrong.

"Why do you say so?" I asked with the liveliest curiosity.

"They didn't build over it, they built next to it, adjacent as you might say. If they'd built over it, they'd have used two walls. You'd have two Roman walls at right angles. You've only got the one, so the Roman fort, if that's what it is, is out to the side of your place, not under it."

I considered this a moment and found it sensible, as I might have expected from Mr Pickering. He went on to make his point clearer. "I'm hazarding the fort was considerably bigger than Seaview. If it was exactly the same size, you'd have four Roman walls in your cellars, of course, but assuming it was bigger, and they were big things, you know, the man building Seaview would have used as much of the foundations as possible, two walls at right angles, and the rest filled in with earth to your own foundations, you see."

I saw very clearly, indeed, and was cheered to know Clavering was wrong. "There's something a bit off about this wall though," Pickering went on. He had my whole attention. "You see how she's set in a mite from the house wall above."

This was seen by following his pointing finger to a small half-window that gave a minimum of light to my cellar. And then I noticed what I had not noticed before. Looking out the window, the house walls jutted a good yard out past the cellar walls. The stones of the outer wall ran to the ground, but the cellar window was recessed to an abnormal degree.

"Odd they'd do that. It weakens the structure somewhat," Pickering went on. "Why wouldn't they have taken the house wall up straight from the Roman foundation? Must be a reason for it."

Only one reason occurred to me. "A secret passage?" I enquired eagerly.

"She'd be a slim one," he informed me, but did not deny the possibility, "And where would she go?" He looked around the cellar for a doorway, but it was clear at a glance there was no secret entrance to the basement. The walls were of uninterrupted stone except for the stairs from the pantry and the window.

"It goes behind this Roman wall into the Roman fort!" I shouted.

He shook his head uncertainly. "You don't find much in the way of a secret passage in these newer homes. In the olden days they had priest's holes and the odd time a passageway into a dungeon, like at Belview, but in these new homes . . ." In historical terms, a house only eighty years old is new.

"It is *possible*?" I asked.

"A very narrow passageway is possible. We'll go above and have a look," he said, and we went at a fast gait up the stairs back to the saloon. My hopes were not high. The panelling looked extremely innocent. Pickering went tapping along the walls with his knuckles this time, listening for hollow sounds, but shook his head despondently. He stopped at the parson's bench, which I informed him sadly did not move. But it interested him. He was convinced it would swing aside to reveal a passageway if only we could find the magic means of movement. We spent the better part of an hour pressing every protuberance anywhere near it. It did not move. Pickering tried then to pull it away by main force, convinced it should come loose, but it was stuck to the wall in some immovable manner. It did not lift, slide right or left, or do a thing but sit as solid as a mountain. At length we had to give it up. I thanked him heartily, paid him, and took him to the kitchen for a glass of ale.

I was more convinced than ever that my house held hidden treasure, and convinced now that it had a secret passage, as well; but when an expert had failed to find it, how should I proceed? There was one who knew more about my house than I knew myself, who had known, for instance, that the parson's bench did not come away from the wall. Clavering I was sure could tell me what I wished to know. I was eager to see him, not because he ever *would* tell me, but because I was looking forward to telling him he was mistaken in the location of the fort, and I also wanted to enquire whether he had managed to cripple the two unfortunate men who wandered into his meadow. He stayed away from us completely, however. Other than the one day we nodded in the village, we did not see him.

CHAPTER
EIGHT

Slack, who must surely have had her book by heart at this point, continued perusing it at every free moment. Sewing, the fire screen, and all other hobbies were neglected. On the Thursday evening we settled in as usual before our fire, Slack with her book, I to work the buttonholes on my riding habit. I had worked on it during the afternoon, and it was done but for the buttonholes.

"Odd the Duke has not been to call all week," Slack mentioned.

"You are eager to discuss Aquae Sulis, I gather?" I asked ironically. "Very likely he is gone to London. He mentioned he was to go soon. Mentioned it quite some time ago."

"Ah, very likely he is gone to Londinium," she said.

I stared at her blightingly. "We have progressed in time to A.D. 1813, Slack. If you mean London, please say so. There is nothing so ill-bred as flaunting your esoteric scraps of knowledge to puff yourself up."

"*You* just said Aquae Sulis," she retaliated, quite childishly.

"You were not used to be so dull you didn't realize when you were being roasted."

"You didn't used to think yourself satirical," she answered sharply.

We might have deteriorated into a squabble, for really Slack was becoming very short-tempered these last days, taking one up on every little thing. We were saved by the sound of the knocker.

"George, and it's only quarter to nine," I said with resignation.

It was not George but Clavering who had decided to honour us with a call, after a week of neglect. I smiled in delight at having a chance to point out to him his error at thinking Willow Hall was built on a fort, and Slack smiled to have at last a fellow antiquarian with whom she might speak her three words of Latin.

The Duke is, of course, about as sensitive as a public bench, but I thought he showed traces of sheepishness at first showing his face after his rude behaviour at Belview. He looked a little self-conscious, unsure of his welcome.

"Ladies," he said, bowing. He was again in black evening clothes, having either been out to dinner or dined in state at home. We both nodded; then he advanced to Slack, offering her a large tin box. Her foolish face beamed with pleasure.

"Why, you're early, Your Grace. My birthday isn't till tomorrow," she chirped.

"Is it indeed? I had no idea. This is not a birthday gift, however, but a replacement for your hospitality the other evening." It was opened to reveal about five pounds of dried cherries. "You mentioned you share my predilection for them," he said. Then he turned to me. "And when I discover if there is anything in this world Miss Denver likes, I shall attempt to bring it to her."

"I am fond of good manners, and would be very happy if you could find some to bring with you next time."

"I would not have guessed it, ma'am," he said with a charming smile. "Do you mind very much if I have a seat?" This was thrown in to remind me of my own lack of manners in not offering him one. I bowed my acquiescence, but he was already seated, with one leg thrown over the other in a vulgar, slouching position.

"Well, and what have the ladies of Seaview been up to recently?" he asked, with a face I did not trust. I felt he had a pretty good notion what we had been up to.

"We have taken up the study of Roman ruins," I said, spurning his thrust regarding Seaview.

"And been making some interesting discoveries, to gather from your smirk," he replied.

"Ladies do not smirk," I pointed out.

"No, *ladies* don't usually," he agreed. "I have never seen Miss Slack, for instance, smirk."

"Might I suggest you take a look at her now," I said, for she was smirking in such a way I longed to shake her.

"I have been reading this book about Aquae Sulis," Slack told him, disdaining to hear my jibe.

"Endlessly," I added, but in a low voice.

"How interesting," Clavering said, turning to face her, so that I had a broad view of a black back, and nothing more but the back of an equally black head. "It is one of the more interesting remains in England," he said, and they were off on a tedious discussion of rectangular baths, round baths, chalybeate springs, arches, Minerva, and so on.

"I always stop a moment when I stand on the diving stone, and look at the groove in it made by all those generations of Romans," he was saying. I sat biding my time, phrasing my own comments to come in the most cutting way possible.

"Oh, have you been there! How I would love to go to Aquae Sulis," Slack declared.

"Why do you not? It is well worth the trip," he said.

"*Some people* are not in the least interested," she said in a meaningful voice, and with a glance at me. "But *I* shall go one day, and to Londinium, too, I have been to Londinium, of course; but not since I have become interested in the Roman ruins, and my book mentions some ruins in Londinium."

"Since that time four days ago, you have not had your head out of the book, Slack. Julius Caesar himself could have been to call, and you would not have known it."

"You must go up to London now that you are aware of its origins," he told her.

"Slack is aware of nothing but Aquae Sulis," I told him. "The book the library had deals with it exclusively."

"London is rich in ruins," the Duke said, turning to hold converse with Slack alone. "Strange, it did not even exist when the Romans landed in England. Colchester was then the capital, if it can even be said there was one. But, of course, the Thames and access to the ocean soon made London the natural capital, and eventually, much later, actually, the governor presided there to administer the four divisions. It is amazing anything remains considering the number of times it was destroyed, and the nearly two thousand years that have passed, but there is still a great deal to see. The London walls, for instance, are still standing in several places, but the best place to see Roman London is from the cellars."

"How interesting," I said in a tone to denote my complete lack of enthusiasm. No one paid me the slightest heed.

"Much of their original pavement is to be seen in shop cellars, and very often a wall, as you have here at Seaview."

I could do nothing but wait patiently while he chatted on to Slack's impressed audience. My moment was coming, and I relished it. He took us on a mental tour along the villas of the Walbrook, the warehouses of the Thames, even to the cemeteries beyond the walls, back to town to admire modern buildings with crooked walls dictated by the Roman ruins on which they were erected, eventually depositing us at the British Museum, to admire reconstructed mosaics, golden jewelry, armour, writing tablets, and other memorabilia, each item of which received an excited "Imagine" or "Really" from Slack.

"I will certainly bear all this in mind when next we go up to Londinium," she assured him.

"In the meanwhile, we have made rather an interesting discovery regarding our own Roman ruins," I said, savouring my triumph.

"Your investigation is causing considerable amuse — interest in town," Clavering said, turning back to me with a certain gloating on his face.

"If the townspeople are amused at my investigation, it is yourself who is to blame, Your Grace, for it is you who misinformed me Willow Hall stands on the ruins of a Roman fort, and it is no such a thing."

"You must confess, ma'am, I never told you a thing about Willow Hall. What I did say is that Seaview is built on one wall of a Roman fort. The other walls, of course, were quite destroyed in the earthquakes that occurred around the time it was built."

"You told me my house stands on a Roman fort!" I said angrily, for I was peeved to have the ground cut out from under my feet, my little triumph destroyed. "You said it would lend a sense of immediacy if tourists could stand on the exact spot where the Roman soldiers looked out to sea!"

"This is the exact spot; it is only that part of the foundations were destroyed."

"You can't know the exact spot if the foundations are gone. Mr Pickering says the Roman fort is adjacent to that wall, out beyond the house."

"Poor Pickering has not had access to the original plans of the house, and the drawings of the Roman fort that accompany it. I planned to put all this material in the museum. You can take my word for it, you stand precisely where the Roman fort stood."

"I never heard of any earthquakes in England."

He stared in astonishment. "Up till 1750 we were prone to them. You *must* have read of the terrible London quakes in 1750. They rocked the city every four weeks for months. There was panic in the streets; the town was all but deserted. Ladies, always on the lookout for a new fashion, had themselves earthquake gowns made up. They occurred a few years earlier here at Pevensey. They were less severe, but they did topple three walls of the Roman fort, unfortunately."

"You're making that up!" I charged.

"I refer you to the excellent and highly readable letters of Mr Horace Walpole. I have a copy of them in my library if you have not, and will be happy to lend them to you."

I was silent. He wouldn't offer proof if none existed, and I was forced to accept it.

"I have read all about the London quakes," Slack told me. "Indeed, I remember Mama speaking of them. Very severe, but I never heard of the Pevensey quakes."

"Neither has anyone else," I muttered.

"But tell me, has there been more trouble with the grate, since you have taken the trouble to have a builder out to investigate?" Clavering asked me.

"Nothing to speak of," I answered with a quelling frown at Slack. I had no desire for her to go telling him I held him to blame, and wouldn't satisfy him to know we were so troubled as we were.

To be fair, she did not tell him he was suspect in the matter, but nothing else was left out of her telling. The awful shakings were all revealed in detail.

"This particular spot is prone to earth tremors. I wonder if that is what causes it," he suggested.

"It wouldn't tremble so violently here and not a single quake felt at Lady Inglewood's or Belview. Have you felt tremors?"

"No, I haven't," he disclaimed at once. "But then Belview was not troubled the other time either, when the Roman fort fell."

"It's something to do with the foundations," I said. "Mr Pickering feels they are irregular. The stone wall is not in the right place. It is set back a yard or more from the line of the house wall, and I am not at all sure there aren't some Roman ruins beyond. Perhaps there is a hole there — water could be seeping in from the sea. Why, the walls might come tumbling down on our heads. I'll do a little excavating there, to the east of the wall, and . . ."

"No!" Clavering said firmly.

"I certainly will!" I answered automatically.

"I think not, Miss Denver. That is *my* land, leased only, and subject to my control. I will not have it dug up. It is just possible there are archaeological remains of interest, and I won't have them botched by an amateur dig."

"Oh, dear me, no," Slack added her appeal at once. "You can't imagine the damage done by the ignorant at Aquae Sulis, Priscilla."

"I am not ignorant, I hope."

"You are ignorant of Roman antiquities. I plan to have it all excavated after you leave, by professionals," Clavering said.

126

"You'll have a long wait!"

"As you pointed out yourself, nineteen years is but a drop in the bucket of time. Still, it is a long time to have to endure the discomfort of a rattling grate and the uncertainty of what causes it. If you wish to sell, I shall begin my excavating at once and solve the mystery."

"You can excavate without my selling. Go ahead. I will be very happy to have it settled."

"No, no. There is no point excavating if we can't dig up under Seaview, as well."

"You said nothing of that. It was to be a museum."

He gave a guilty start. "That decision had not actually been taken, that we would do any excavating. It is an alternative plan, but in any case the house would not have been torn down. A careful dig in the cellar would be possible if no one were actually living here."

"Oh, you're as slippery as an eel! I know perfectly you're up to something," I said in exasperation.

He looked at me as though I had run mad. "You know what I am up to. I make no secret of it."

"You make it so confusing there is no understanding it. First you want the house for your aunt, then for a museum, then to dig up."

"I explained that."

"If you choose to consider further confusion explanation. But there is another little mystery that bothers me. I saw two men disappear into your meadow the other day, and when I went after them to warn them . . ."

"You didn't go into that trapped meadow!" he bellowed.

"Yes, I did, and escaped quite intact, unlike the poor man at the inn. But as I was saying I went, *very carefully*, in after them to warn them, and they had vanished. Could you throw any light on the matter, Your Grace, for it troubles me excessively that two grown men should quite vanish before my eyes?"

"I don't quite understand you," he said, narrowing his eyes in a suspicious way. "You were following them, and they disappeared?"

"No, I was not actually there when it happened. I saw them from the attic window and went after them, on Juliette, but when I got to the meadow, they were gone."

"Ah, I think I know what you speak of now. I had a couple of chaps in to begin clearing out the foundations for the reconstruction work I spoke of. Very likely it was they you saw. They came on along to Belview to speak to me about it."

"On wings, I must conclude, since they left no trace in the tall grass. Their trail stopped at the chapel."

He wagged a finger at me playfully. "There is more than traps to be feared in the meadows, Miss Denver. They must have hidden in the foundation, with a view to frightening you, or worse. I really would advise very strongly you stay out of that area."

"I looked in the foundations."

He tensed, hardly perceptibly, but his body stiffened. "And what did you find?"

"Nothing. I'm sure they were not hiding there."

The tenseness was gone, and he turned playful in relief, "You have your ghosts in the chimney, and now it seems I have phantoms in my meadow. One and the same, do you think?"

"I doubt either ghosts or phantoms have much to do with either one, but that is not to say there isn't some connection."

"What do you conceive to be the link?" he asked, but before I was required to invent one, Slack, who had been unwrapping her cherries, passed the box to Clavering, and the subject of ghosts was forgotten. Clavering passed the box on to me, but I detest sticky sweet cherries nearly as much as these two relish them, and pushed them away.

"Priscilla likes dates," Slack told him.

"So you had Juliette in the meadow. How do you two go on?" he asked.

"We are coming to terms. I don't clutch her reins and she doesn't throw me. I have been around the garden dozens of times and am ready to essay a larger field."

"You are welcome to use the spinney as I told you before. I think you are foolish to learn to ride on such a spirited mount, and advise you strongly not to go out unaccompanied. I frequently take a ride in the afternoon and would be happy to go with you."

I had not the least idea of revealing my scanty progress to him and declined the offer, so he returned to his other flirt, Slack.

"So your birthday is coming up, Miss Slack? I expect you have a large party planned."

"No, indeed, at my age I am past all that," she told him, smiling fondly.

"Nonsense, till you reach fifty, in five or ten years, you should celebrate every one, and at fifty, of course, you turn the calendar around and progress backward, celebrating more strenuously than ever."

Slack was incensed when I later accused her of tittering, but a titter is what her reaction sounded like to me. Clavering had found his way back into her affections with a box of dried cherries and an insincere compliment on her juvenescence. Aquae Sulis and Londinium helped, but it was the compliment about her age that got her to run for the wine and macaroons.

"Making yourself a new gown?" he asked, after she had left. I was working on my buttonholes throughout his visit. I saw no need to assume a ladylike idleness.

"No, a riding habit."

"May I see it?" he asked, which I considered amazingly impertinent. He appeared not to notice my displeasure but lifted it from my fingers to hold up and examine.

"Very nice. The colour will suit you," he said, looking from the bottle green jacket to my hair, eyes, and face.

"It is not beauty but serviceability I am interested in," I replied.

"Still, you have chosen well. And executed well, too. A very fine stitch." I can only assume he was short-sighted. This, without Slack's help, was the worst piece of clothing I had ever turned out. "Are you sure you wouldn't like to ride with me? I am considered a good rider."

"I'm sure you are, but such skills must be acquired, not brushed on by one who possesses them, like a coat of paint."

"Is the whole of the teaching profession mistaken, then, if skills cannot be taught? Who is teaching you? Lord Inglewood?"

"He has helped me a little."

"He is good. You should progress quickly under his tutelage if you have any aptitude for it at all."

I did not feel it necessary to tell him George had helped me only the once and that I had no aptitude whatsoever. He picked up Slack's book about Bath and thumbed through it. "You take no interest at all in this?" he asked.

"I am learning, interested or not."

"It is a fascinating study, you know. We are ideally situated here, with many of their works still visible without even digging. Would you and Miss Slack not be interested to take a drive over to Porchester Castle one day? And closer to home, I have an excellent library at Belview. I hope you and Miss Slack will feel free to use it. My librarian will be happy to help you."

"I will be sure to tell Miss Slack. It is her hobby, not mine."

He told her himself when she returned a moment later about the library, but did not mention the visit to Porchester Castle. Perhaps I flatter myself, but I wondered whether he didn't fear he would be stuck to take her alone, since I think I had made it clear I had but little interest in his fascinating study. Her joy reached a new peak. She couldn't press the cherries, macaroons, and wine on him hard enough or fast enough. I think it was her insistence that caused him to leave not much later.

I arose to walk to the hall with him, from a sense of politeness merely, since he had been fairly civil this evening. "About Porchester . . ." he began, as soon as we were out of the saloon.

"Oh, would you like to ask Miss Slack?" I enquired in an innocent voice.

He clenched his lips and frowned. "I'm not a leper, you know," he said.

"No, indeed! She would be perfectly safe with you."

"Good night, Miss Denver."

"Good night, Your Grace."

I went back to the saloon, laughing under my breath.

Slack was in alt. "Very civil of him," she enthused. "Free rein of his library at any time. And he is usually quite standoffish, you know. Lady Ing has not been to Belview above half a dozen times, in all the years she has lived here."

"Yes, he means to flatter us well, to be rid of us. That is what all his civility is about, Slack. Make no mistake about that."

"I would have liked to ask him to my birthday party," she said.

"But then we would have to limit the number of candles, would we not? Write him a note, if you wish to ask him. It is your party."

"Oh, I wouldn't like to do that. Very likely he is busy. He always wears evening clothes when he comes in the evening. If he doesn't go out, he must have friends in.

132

He wouldn't dress to dine alone. He would have his plans ready by now; I've left it too late."

She was wrong, for he came uninvited, and behaved so abominably I blush to write it. When I was in my bed, I realized that I had let him go away with no real explanation for the men who had disappeared in his meadow. I couldn't but wonder if they had been wounded; and he at pains to conceal it from me, for I doubt many had ever accused him to his face of selfishness and cruelty. There was still no explanation for my grate, either. Nothing had been resolved, and it was difficult to account for the strange feeling of contentment that hung about me.

CHAPTER
NINE

The day of Slack's party dawned fair and clear, a truly beautiful day. I made a quick trip into town without her in the morning (no easy thing in the usual way, but I imagine she suspected the nature of it) to fetch her present. The books we had ordered had not yet come in, but I had her other present to bring back. I had got her a diamond ring. It is, of course, an extravagant gift, a thing I do not possess myself; but she has been with me forever and is not likely to acquire one by any other means. Every woman ought at some time in her life to own a diamond ring. Also, Slack has particularly lovely hands, the fingers long and graceful. Prior to this most recent madness for archaeology she used to spend a good deal of her time at stitchery of one form or another, and the diamond would be well shown off on her. It was not a great gaudy thing, one carat actually, but it cost a good deal and was likely, I hoped, to give us both much pleasure. I wore a smile as I set out for home with it in my reticule.

There was a caller at Willow Hall during my absence, that is to say, he came during my absence, and was still there when I returned. It was Mr McMaster, no favourite these days with Slack due his having brought his open carriage for the drive to Eastbourne. No dried cherries for him, but at least a glass of wine, I was relieved to see.

"What brings you out our way?" I enquired, in a spirit of friendship only, not vulgar curiosity.

"I had to make a call at Belview and, as I was so close, wanted to say hello to you and Miss Slack."

I was eager to hear what took him to Belview, but could not like to ask. But he was a good talker and was soon telling us.

"Our kitchen girl is leaving us, getting married, and we are looking for a replacement. Young Mary Hinks would like to come to us, but her parents are separated, her father works at Belview, and I must get his approval, though she doesn't live with him. He was happy enough to be rid of her. She will come to us shortly now. They had a spot of trouble at Belview while I was there. Billie McCormick gave his leg a hit while chopping wood, and the place was in an uproar. But the Duke is very good in an emergency. The men were running in circles and the women weeping into their aprons, but the Duke put a tourniquet on him and rushed him into town, to the doctor. The leg will be all right, thank God, and in the meanwhile, of course, His Grace will give the family every support. Financial support, I mean. He takes very good care of his own people."

"A pity he couldn't see his way fit to give Leo Milkin at the inn some financial support," I said. I was happy to hear Clavering had some traces of decent feelings in his makeup.

"That character?" McMaster said, and let out a ring of laughter. "He was Clavering's pensioner for over a year after he hurt his ankle in that mantrap. He is no more crippled than you or I, Miss Denver. He can walk as well as anyone but puts on his limp when he gets a gullible customer at the inn, and tells his sad story about feeding his family, and he not even married. It is all an act to get a sizable *pourboire*. Don't be taken in by him."

As I already had been, I allowed the matter to drop but was fully aware of the speaking glances flashed at me by Slack, as though to say, "*Now* you see who was right." She could hardly wait to get McMaster out the door before she faced me with it, but when she took to puffing Clavering up as a Good Samaritan, she tried my patience too far.

"Paying Leo Milkin some paltry pension for a year after crippling him is hardly the act of a Good Samaritan. It goes some *small* way toward mitigating the evil, and the fact that Milkin himself is a scoundrel, little better than a common thief, doesn't change anything."

"The McCormick man, too — Mr McMaster mentioned it quite as a matter of course that Clavering would see to his family while he can't work. He always takes good care of his people, Mr McMaster said."

"If he took *good* care of them, they wouldn't be wounding themselves in his service. The man was likely fagged to death, being overworked."

"He wouldn't have been fagged in the *morning*," Slack pointed out. I saw at once that argument was

136

useless and desisted, for I did not wish to spoil this special day with bickering.

As the diamond ring exceeded what we usually exchange in the way of a gift, the occasion became something out of the ordinary, and I was planning to dress up in my new green silk, as yet unworn. The fact of the material's having been brought in by the smugglers enhanced the attraction of the gown in my eyes. I felt quite a renegade when I put it on, a little reckless with my naked white shoulders peeping out where I was accustomed to see decent cloth. It was, I suppose, Clavering's remark that my green riding habit suited me that made me think of him as I turned in front of my mirror, admiring myself. I felt a little sorry he wouldn't be seeing the outfit, though it was not the same shade of green as the riding habit he had liked, not "Paddy green," as Slack described it, but a pretty, deep green, darker than the leaf of an apple tree. The green, more or less, of a walnut tree's leaf. A sparkling stone would have set it off to great advantage, but I possessed none, and hung my pearls around my neck. I thought I looked quite elegant, and when Slack saw me, she thought so, too.

She wore her best black crape, looking every inch the mourner, but black is her colour, and there was no point chiding her for it. Lady Inglewood in purple and George in evening dress came at six o'clock. We usually dined at this hour, but for the party we were putting it off till seven, to lengthen the evening a bit, and were sitting like civilised persons having a glass of wine when the knocker sounded. No one came in, but a parcel was handed over for Slack, creating a very pleasant diversion. We knew it was not the Inglewoods' present; they had brought a box with them, which sat coyly on a table, not yet given over, and therefore presumably invisible to us all, as we tried to keep our heads from turning in its direction. This was a larger parcel, and when the paper was torn off, it was seen to be a broken statue.

There was only one person in the neighbourhood who would consider a broken piece of statuary a suitable gift. "Clavering!" I said, and erupted into hoydenish laughter. "It serves you well for pretending to like such stuff. Slack," I teased her.

She refused to take offence at either the gift or my words, but turned the thing around this way and that, trying to make out what it represented. It was in terra cotta (I think — a brownish red clay, in any case) and was of a young person, whether male or female there was no saying. The young person held out a hand from which suspended some very small ball on a string, at a very odd angle. The person was seated, admiring the ball. It was very odd and not well executed in my opinion, but Slack was vastly pleased with it. Or with the notion of receiving a gift from the Duke, in any case.

"What — how should Clavering know it is her birthday?" Lady Inglewood demanded at once, and very riled she was, too, that we should be on such terms of intimacy as to be getting gifts from him.

"Why, we told him last night when he called, Aunt Ethelberta," I had the exquisite pleasure of informing her, and was soon at pains to let her know Clavering had not come empty-handed last night, either. "He brought Slack down a box of dried cherries. They are both very fond of them."

"I hadn't realized His Grace ran quite tame here," Lady Ing said at once. "You mentioned nothing of this to me."

"I have mentioned various times that he comes to see us, and you knew, of course, that he had us to Belview."

"It is all business, you said. You didn't tell me he was running over every night with a present."

"Oh, the presents are not for *me*; it is only Slack he gives gifts to. If you disapprove of him as her flirt, you must speak to her."

"Pooh! If he is haunting the place in this fashion, it is yourself he is interested in, not Slack."

I thought it was only our making social headway with such an exalted personage as His Grace that piqued her, but soon realized she saw in him a rival for my hand, a rival for George, I mean. Her next remark, though seeming to denote the contrary, made it quite obvious. "Don't think you have a chance in the world of landing him, Priscilla. It is no such a thing. He will never marry a local girl, certainly not a schoolteacher's daughter, but will make some great match with an heiress in London."

"You hear that, Slack? You must look lively," I cautioned playfully.

My aunt gave George a look that commanded him to take a seat by my side and get busy making love to me, and till dinner was ready I had a bad time of it. She spoke to Slack about Clavering's present, hefting the statue, turning it upside down and telling her at last that it was just some old thing he had found lying about, and it was really an insult. When I began to hear Slack speak of Aquae Sulis, I turned my full attention to George and let him woo me with talk of some new gun he had bought, or was going to buy — his speaking of a gun is really all I recall — and had uphill work making it sound like romance to his mother. Dinner was finer and fancier than we normally took, and after eating I proposed a toast to Slack, handing over her ring. She cried when she saw what it was. I felt a perfect fool, and Aunt Ethelberta's eyes were sparking with anger. Really it was an extraordinarily uncomfortable interlude, but Slack loved her present, and that made it worthwhile.

"I didn't realize diamonds were the order of the day," Lady Ing said, handing Slack her box with a very poor grace. It was a netting box, which brought no tears of joy, but was received graciously and might prove useful in days to come once the novelty of Roman ruins wore off. We then removed to the saloon, where I hoped — half hoped — we would not be troubled by our grate. I would not have been totally unhappy to let my aunt see that it did indeed perform stunts, but on that occasion it was as quiet as a grate ought to be. The birthday party was as well as over. No very baroque entertainment to be sure, but not unenjoyable. It was nine o'clock, and though it was the hour at which George often arrived, I could see that both he and his mama were rehearsing to take their leave, and was not sorry, either. But before they managed to invent an

140

excuse for leaving so early — no more than a few yawns had been indulged in yet — the knocker sounded. As George sat before my eyes, I suspected it was Clavering.

"That will be His Grace," Slack said, and jumped up to run into the hall in her eagerness to thank him for the gift.

"Does he come that often, then?" Lady Ing asked me, her eyes like saucers.

"No, certainly not," I told her and said no more, for I could hear Slack thanking him, and his deep voice replying. They entered immediately, stopping in the archway. He bowed to Lady Ing and me, nodded to George, and entered.

"How maladroit of me, bursting in on a family party," he said, then turned to Slack. "You most particularly told me you were not entertaining this evening. Miss Slack, or I would not have come bothering you. There is nothing so unwanted as an uninvited guest, but I disliked to have your birthday pass without wishing you well."

"We were going to ask you to come, too, but were sure you would be busy," she gushed back.

"You were wrong," he said, leaning toward her and waving a finger under her nose. "I dined alone, thinking of you, and would have been delighted to come. So, you liked the statuette?"

"Immoderately!" she breathed happily.

"The subject is particularly appropriate for us two cherryphiles. That was a bunch of cherries the little boy held, but unfortunately only one remains."

"So that's what it is! I thought it was a tiny little ball," she told him, with a proud smile toward me to show me how she had him under her thumb. Really, it was better than a farce to watch her carry on with a man young enough to be her son.

"Lady Inglewood and George gave me this handsome netting box," she said, picking it up to show him.

"Very nice. Now tell me the big news. Which of your beaux gave you that diamond you are flashing around? Out with it, Miss Slack. I know you have relented and accepted an offer from one of your court. Who is he, so that I may begin hating him?"

She was pink and puffed with pleasure. "Miss Denver gave it to me. I don't know what possessed her to waste such a sum. I am very angry with her," she said, with a broad smile in my direction.

"I got ahead of you!" I told him. "But you had your chance."

"One of your own many leftovers?" he quizzed. "You really ought not to accept the ring unless you mean to have the gentleman, as well."

He came in and sat down between George and myself, and proceeded to flirt outrageously with Slack and me. I was about to say I don't know what my aunt thought of his performance, but she did know, or thought she did. She thought he was my beau and was incensed at his cutting George out.

"You will be putting George's nose out of joint with talk of my niece accepting diamond rings from gentlemen, Your Grace," she said, with a nod in our

142

direction. How she put so much expression into a nod is difficult to explain. It said more loudly than words, this pair are matched. Don't go trying to make mischief between them.

Clavering looked at me with a laughing question in his black eyes. "Indeed! I hadn't realized that was the way the wind blows. But I should have known when Miss Denver is so elegantly attired to entertain her cousin that there was romance in the air. She does not bother to dress up for *me*, you see."

"I am dressed up for Slack's birthday party," I said to the door, for I didn't feel up to looking at either of them.

"And looking very well, ma'am, if I neglected to mention it," Clavering said.

George, I believe, must have received a mute blast from his mama's direction, for he, too, said, "Yes, Cousin, dashed fine."

"Thank you, George."

"You didn't thank *me*," the Duke pointed out.

"Thank you."

"You are most welcome." He bowed formally, only his eyes revealing that all this was a charade, pure and simple.

"How does friend grate go on?" he asked next. "Not likely to take a leap at me tonight, I trust?"

"No, it has been behaving well since I threatened it with Mr Pickering."

I had not mentioned his coming to Aunt Ethelberta, so she took the idea I was keeping things from her, also the idea that Clavering was completely in our pocket.

143

"What's this? What's all this about Mr Pickering? It seems to me you are wasting a deal of money, Priscilla, buying extravagant presents for servants and . . ."

"Miss Slack is not a servant."

"Well, she is not family."

"We consider Slack family," Clavering said in a proprietary way, with one of his damned winks at Slack, which was not unobserved by my aunt. I don't know what he was up to, unless it was plain perverse pleasure in discomfiting me.

"Do *we* indeed?" she asked him, in a tone of heavy irony.

"Yes, we do!" I told her, not to defend Clavering, but because I was so angry with her for offending Slack. "And she *is* family, related to Papa." Actually she was only a tenuous connection.

"Do *we* also feel it necessary for Mr Pickering to come and look at the grate?" my aunt asked the Duke, her nose pinched in displeasure.

"Do you know, the ladies did it without consulting me?" he replied, behaving quite as irately as she was herself at our independence. "You'd think the place was their own and they were answerable to no one. Becoming very headstrong, these girls of ours. It's time we trimmed them back into line."

Lady Ing was bereft of speech, a unique occurrence in all my dealings with her. Clavering spoke on uninterrupted. "And while we are in the midst of this pleasant little family discussion, I mean to take you to task for selling Priscilla that wild nag, Lady Inglewood."

This was going too far, a "Priscilla" on top of "these girls of ours," as though he actually were a relative and not a virtual stranger. "Really!" I gasped, staring at him.

"You are about to tell me you can manage your own affairs, Priscilla," he want on calmly, "but you can't, you know. You'll come to grief on that nag yet."

"I don't see it's anyone's business but our own if my niece and I arrange a bargain between us," Lady Ing told him, recovering her speech.

"I take a strong interest in your niece, ma'am, George notwithstanding, and I object," he answered reasonably.

"Well, you may go to the devil!" I told him bluntly, about fed up with his officiousness.

"All in good time," he agreed blandly, while Lady Ing nodded her head in vigorous agreement with my words.

"Don't you think Juliette is too wild for your cousin, George?" Clavering asked, turning to include George in the family squabble.

"She's full of juice," was George's answer.

"Certainly she is, but I still don't think she can handle Juliette."

"He didn't mean *me*! He meant the horse," I said angrily.

"Forgive me. It was meant as a compliment, Priscilla. Ought I to have said full of pluck?"

"George is teaching her to ride," Lady Ing said.

"Yes, I have been told George has the monopoly in *that* sphere," Clavering replied mischievously.

"He will make certain nothing happens to her, and if you can't handle Juliette, Priscilla dear, I'm sure you

145

have only to tell me, and we will make some other arrangement."

"I can handle her."

I suggested a glass of wine to bring harmony to the meeting, but achieved only a brief peace. "Let us propose a toast to Miss Slack," the Duke suggested. "Happy birthday, my dear, and may you have many more of them."

This was well enough, except for the "my dear," but his next speech threw my aunt quite into a fit. "When do we take that trip to Aquae Sulis, Miss Slack?" he asked.

"Eh, what is this? You aren't taking a trip with the Duke, Miss Slack? It is entirely unseemly," Lady Ing flared up.

"Not in the least, Priscilla will chaperone us," he told her.

"He is joking, Aunt," I said, with a glare at the joker.

"It seems a pretty funny joke to me."

"Oh, but jokes are supposed to be funny, you know," he pointed out.

"Well it isn't funny," she snapped.

"It is a woman's prerogative to change her mind. I didn't see any humour in it myself. When do we go, Miss Slack?"

"I am more interested in going to Belview to visit your library, since you were kind enough to offer," Slack replied, with more diplomacy than I would have given her credit for. But it was a fresh offence to my aunt that we should have the run of Clavering's library.

146

"We have all kinds of books at Inglewood. I'm sure you are welcome to read them," she told Slack.

"It is literature on Roman ruins that particularly interests us," Clavering said.

"It is news to me that Miss Slack is interested in anything of the sort. She never opened a book at Inglewood, nor so much as looked at onc of my husband's coins or shards."

"Your late husband had but an indifferent collection, ma'am," he remarked. "She will do better to come to me."

I could see my aunt wouldn't take much more of this without coming to cuffs, possibly outright blows. When she looked at her watch and said it was getting late, I didn't stir a finger to detain her. "Time we *all* should be going," she said again, with an imperative glare at Clavering.

"I stay up past half past nine myself, and if memory serves, you ladies do not retire with the hens, either; but don't let us detain *you*, Lady Inglewood," he answered, arising to see her out. Not just politely arising in deference to a lady's doing so, but actually taking her elbow and piloting her toward the door, quite firmly, with a look over his shoulder to garner in George.

"I'll speak to you tomorrow, Priscilla," she said. *Speak to you*, not *see you*, and the tone told the manner in which she would speak, a lecture.

"You've been warned," he said aside to me, but in no low voice.

Lady Ing heard and glared.

"Don't stay up too late," my aunt cautioned as she left.

"We *are* celebrating Miss Slack's birthday," Clavering reminded her. And after the Inglewoods had left, we celebrated it much more pleasantly, too, with more wine, quite a good deal of it.

"What was the meaning of that performance, Clavering?" I asked bluntly.

"Always happy to oblige a lady in distress."

"I was not in distress prior to your arrival."

"You are in distress one way or the other, my girl. If you want George, you need to give him some competition. Really, you know, he ain't half convinced to have you. And if you don't, I will make an excellent excuse to turn him off. Oh, I know I'm ugly as sin and twice as reprehensible, but I'm the richest gent in the parish."

"How nice for you."

"It softens the blow of having a face only a mother could love," he said, looking at me with his bold, black, gypsy eyes.

Slack made some clucking demurs to this self-insult; I did not, for what he said was true enough.

"Don't you agree?" he asked, point-blank.

"Yes."

He threw back his head and laughed. "Well, you're frank anyway."

"I see no reason to mince words. You are darker than is stylish this year."

"Or any other year, except possibly in Africa. I must say, however, personal vanity is not one of my failings."

148

I made no reply to this, and he went on to add in a spirit of pure malice, "Nor yours either, I think? This is the first time I have ever seen you dressed up a little."

It was the "a little" that rankled. I had never been more dressed up in my life. "And a lady who gives diamonds to her friends when she does not wear them herself surely sets a precedent for lack of vanity that will rarely be equalled."

"I don't quite shower them over all my friends. Slack is more than a friend to me. Well, she is a diamond herself, and a more valuable one than the stone she wears."

"I couldn't agree with you more. But we are causing our diamond to blush, become a rose diamond. Forgive us, Miss Slack. Next time we wish to puff you up, we shall take care you don't overhear us. The more sensitive amongst us dislike praise. I am not so sensitive myself." He stopped and looked around at us. "I see no one means to try me with a compliment. I was once told I had nice hands — by a sculptor, too, and he should know. But they are not so diamond-worthy as Miss Slack's. You have elegant hands, Miss Slack."

Slack was wriggling with embarrassment, and I wished to change the subject for her sake. Personally I would rather be abused to my face any day than hear praise, and I know she is the same. Repeated, second-hand praise is fine, but not to the face.

"We heard you had a little trouble at Belview today?" I remarked. "Mr McMaster stopped in and told us about Bill McCormick. How is he?"

"He'll do. The blood was flowing quite freely, but the bone wasn't touched. Mr McMaster, you say, told you?"

"Yes, he stopped in on his way home."

"But Seaview isn't on his way home."

"Well, it is not far out of his way," I pointed out.

"Planning another trip to Eastbourne?" he asked, with a sly smile. "I wonder what the attraction is at Eastbourne, when Porchester does not draw you at all."

"It's the open carriage, Your Grace," Slack explained. "Mr McMaster always brings his open carriage, to ensure *my* staying at home, you see."

"He's not such a slow top as I thought," Clavering said, then looked around the room, as though searching for something. "You have no pianoforte here. What a pity; it would go well on this festive occasion, and soothe this savage breast, too. Why have you no pianoforte, Priscilla? The food of love is quite lacking here."

"I should get one; Miss Slack plays very well," I replied, suppressing any mention of cherries as a suitable substitute for music in fuelling love.

"I have a clavichord at home that no one plays," he said. "Since getting the pianoforte, the clavichord has been consigned to a dark corner, unused, and probably completely out of tune, while the pianoforte has the place of honour, also unused and out of tune. If you would like to have the use of the clavichord, I will have it shipped down."

"Now that is poorly done of you, Your Grace! Having an instrument to while away our evenings will only encourage us to stay about. You'll never be rid of us," I cautioned, while wondering furiously what he was up to.

"You notice I didn't offer the pianoforte. I'm hedging my bets; but as you seem determined to stay, we might as well have some music. And my friends call me Burne, by the way."

"What an odd name!" I said.

"Short for Wedderburne, my first name. Actually another last name, Mama's, but I had the misfortune to inherit it as a Christian name."

"Sounds heathen," Slack said, "Burne."

"Quite like an injunction to incinerate myself; but I prefer it to being regularly ordered to Wed, which is the alternative," he explained.

"You aren't in favour of marriage, then?" Slack asked.

"While there are housetops to jump from, I don't see why anyone commits the folly. But then the human race dotes on torturing itself. Ladies lace and ride sidesaddle and do needlework, and gentlemen go to Parliament and waltz and shave. And most of this torture, barring Parliament, is designed to make ourselves attractive to the other sex, so that we might achieve the ultimate folly of marriage. Very odd when one considers it, is it not?" he asked with a sardonic smile, thinking to engage us in a futile argument.

"Very odd," I said quickly, before Slack could enter on a defence of marriage. "But I thought you involved yourself in Parliament."

"I do. We must all satisfy our little urge to self-flagellation, and it is the least likely to make me a husband."

"You won't get any argument from me," Slack said, "I have no opinion of it either." I don't know whether she said this in a mistaken idea that it would please him to agree, or to create the illusion she could have married had she chosen, but in any case it surprised me, and it surprised the Duke, too.

"And you, Miss Denver, do you, too, agree with me?" he asked.

"Absolutely. Especially I think ladies are foolish to marry if they don't have to, for the advantage is all the man's. *He* continues free as a bird, but she becomes an unpaid *housekeeper* and bearer of children, while losing control of her fortune."

He blinked twice and looked from one of us to the other. "She gains a protector, and a certain position in society. The advantage is not all the man's. What would become of the human race if everyone thought as *you* do?"

"It would die out, of course, and good riddance, too," I replied calmly. "Nine-tenths of the people one meets are worthless. People by and large destroy the paradise God created. It should be left to the birds and bees and animals who appreciate it. You don't see them ruining the air with coal dust, nor making war on each other, nor laying mantraps . . ."

"I never heard such nonsense!" he said, taking the woman's prerogative and changing his mind.

"Indeed? But surely it is an extension of your own view. Or did you have in mind some means of continuing procreation without benefit of marriage? I almost think that would be worse than anything. Children running wild, with no parents nor home to curb them, nor family unit to raise them as civilised people."

He settled back with a satisfied smile and continued to argue the point from whichever point of view suited him and made lively discussion. For an hour we discussed half-formed theories of raising children in houses with paid guardians, while the adult population ran about, the men unshaved and the women unlaced, both free to do pretty well as they pleased. His Utopia sounded considerably like Sodom and Gomorrah, with clothing being abandoned entirely at one point, except for the cold weather; but it was all a conceited tease to try to shock Slack and me, who sat impassive, adding such ideas as occurred to us. Slack expressed some interest in changing her skirts for trousers, which led me to comment that it was my desire to be rid of my curls and have convenient short tresses like a man. Clavering had more trouble than we in hiding his horror at these notions, but would not for the world say so. We drank a good deal of wine, those two devoured many dried cherries, and before he left, the Duke also had a piece of Slack's birthday cake. He urged us to go to his library *ad lib*, promised he would send down the clavichord as soon as he had it tuned, and finally left.

"He's an interesting talker, I'll say that for him," Slack said when he was gone.

"He's as crooked as a dog's hind leg," I added. "He thinks to become our friend and get Willow Hall from us. You catch more flies with honey than with vinegar, but he won't catch us."

"I wonder," Slack said, and laughed archly.

CHAPTER
TEN

The next morning Slack went in the carriage to borrow books on Roman antiquities, and I remained home to deal alone with Lady Inglewood, who came to inform me I was wasting my time decking myself out in harlot's gear — no, I do not exaggerate. That was her word — to win the Duke of Clavering. I told her we shared the common view, my paramour and I, that marriage was for fools, which so enraged her that she left before I could tell her about the clavichord; but I did throw in as she left that Slack was even then at his house, arranging the evening's trysting place. The visit had the unfortunate effect of increasing George's calls on us to win me back from Clavering's malign views on marriage, and to spy and see just how much time he actually spent with us and whether I was chaperoned, I imagine. I put him to good use in my lessons and was beginning to feel quite an expert horsewoman. Other than putting on an occasional spurt of uncontrollable speed that terrified me, Juliette was coming under my control. The reins no longer felt like harness straps between my fingers, though I was still not convinced the popular arrangement was the optimum one.

Slack's conversation, what there was of it, became almost totally incomprehensible to me as she progressed into the esoterica of antiquity. She lost all interest in any period later than A.D. 200 and reverted to the terminology of the era of her new interest. Londinium and Aquae Sulis were now familiar to me, but Anderida was a mystery for some time, till I eventually learned by induction it was none other than our own Pevensey. Rutapiae and Camulodunum were substituted for Richborough and Colchester, while her only concern with the countryside was to determine whether a little hump in the earth housed a barrow — a burial mound — and whether a stone wall or stretch of road were old enough to be praised. She took to roaming the park with her head bent looking for "artifacts," and imagining she had found them in bent nails, rusty saucepan handles, and hairpins. When at home her nose was in one of Clavering's books. I spoke in vain of a new Persian carpet for the saloon, and of putting in a hedge to protect us from the dust of the road, and as to mending the sheets — well! An antiquarian had better things to do with her time.

Clavering gave her every encouragement in this new hobby. He came often at night to peruse the books with her. They were now just plain Burne and Slack to each other, all formality abandoned. I became "Prissie" to them both, a name I abhor. I occasionally called Clavering "Wed" to annoy him, but when he once remarked, "I begin to get the idea," I ceased. There, my pen is broken, and I shall discontinue this and take a stroll along the beach.

This next section, you will notice, is written in a different hand than Miss Denver's scrawl. It is being written by me, Miss Slack. I have a first name, incidentally, a detail that has thus far been omitted. It is Maude, and Burne calls me Maude, not Slack. He pointed out to me that I was not slack at all, meaning inactive, negligent, and a host of other dilatory things. He is very quick to make a joke of such things. Miss Denver pointed out that she is not prissy either — prim, prudish — but we call her it in fun, since she never ceases to rise to the bait. I have had the opportunity to peruse her story thus far (I do occasionally glance at some other writing than Burne's books) and feel impelled to point out that it is riddled with inaccuracies, to say nothing of questionable grammar. It presents a very biased view of the events and particularly of my own part in them. Going back some little way in her tale, I might say that I am not in the least afraid of men, and particularly masculine men, as she redundantly describes them. I do dislike rude, boorish men, which Burne is not, and if it appeared to her I was fond of George, it was only to conceal her own Turkish treatment of him.

I have been accused of stuffing Burne with cherries and wine, but I see it was not mentioned that after the first time he had them at our house, she purchased the very next day a large tin herself, and she loathes them. Nor did she give them to me but set them on the table in the saloon. I leave it to your imagination to work out why. There is also a little tampering with the truth

157

regarding my actions when Clavering was present. She would have you believe I was fawning on him, which I was never with anyone in my life. When the titular hostess sits as mute as a chair and glares at a guest, I feel it incumbent on myself to make some conversation. Her behaviour in his presence was from the beginning peculiar in the extreme. She wishes to give the impression she had no feeling other than loathing for the man, but the fact is, she was smitten. From the first day he brought her home after her tumble she was in love, and I say with no other motive than kindness that her subsequent farouche behaviour in his presence was due to this. He is not handsome, to be sure a little darker than the ideal, but with very nice eyes and a particularly winning smile. Her chagrin and her behaviour were due to the fact that the feeling was not reciprocated. He came certainly at first to try to get her to sell him Seaview, which she herself calls Seaview on any occasion when Burne is not present or under discussion. I think his present rash of visits has nothing to do with Seaview, and certainly very little to do with myself and my new hobby. I am not foolish enough to think a duke of thirty years has any romantic interest in me. In fact, my remark, questioned by Miss Denver, that I disapprove of marriage is true, insofar as it applies to myself. A fifty-one-year-old spinster must be a ninny to think of it as still a possible alternative, and, in any case, I am very happy with Priscilla.

The only impediment to the arrangement is that I do absolutely nothing to earn my salary. I am a companion paid handsomely for living in a fine home with a young lady who feels it appropriate to give me a diamond ring for my birthday. However, if I left, she would have to hire someone else, and as we have gone on comfortably together for so many years, I have no intention of leaving *yet*. An event might occur in the forseeable future that would make my companionship unnecessary. I'll say no more.

It has been hinted that my interest in Roman ruins is spurious. It is far from being the case. I do not simulate this interest to make up to Burne, but have fortunately at this late stage in my life found a hobby of consuming interest, and spend much time reading up on it. The hobby has found *me*, Burne says, as it found him. If I occasionally say Anderida instead of Pevensey, it is because I have so often read it, and one begins to speak automatically in the terms frequently encountered. Priscilla would have you believe she herself takes no interest in all this, but I have more than once found a book I was reading missing, and discovered it later turned to a different page. I cannot think Wilkins, the butler, shares my hobby, and the servant girl cannot read. It was my intention to teach her, and still is, but I find I have little spare time to do so. Actually, I have begun writing up an extract on the ruins around Pevensey, and though it has not been mentioned, I am frequently addressed nowadays as Doctor Slack by my employer.

The firescreen sits abandoned, nor has one been brought down from the attics. I must find a moment to go up and look it over and see if it will do. That was an ill-judged start, the day she ran from the attic to the

159

meadow without telling me, and might have got maimed very easily. Odd about those two men she saw, who disappeared. But the grate no longer rattles, and our little mystery is nearly forgotten. But I was saying I have abandoned the firescreen. It sits in the corner with exactly five square inches worked, and it will stand there unless Priscilla decides to finish it. This is unlikely in the extreme; she is awkward with her needle, poor soul. Never had the knack of it, in spite of my best efforts to teach her. It took her an eternity to finish her riding habit without my help, and truth, to tell, it gapes at the neck, though I do not tell her so. She is very sensitive about her appearance these days. The green silk, to spite me cut lower and tighter than is modest, has been put on twice since the birthday party, and though it is nowhere mentioned, there have been two more trips to Anderida where a modiste is this minute making up a gown in rose satin and another in white with a thin red stripe, very pretty. She has also gone to have her hair styled and bought new patent slippers. The reason given is that we are now moving in higher circles than formerly. This is true, and it is quite shocking the short shrift all our other friends have got in this chronicle. Mr McMaster for instance, was pretty well acknowledged as a beau before the advent of Burne, but now he is played down as hardly even an acquaintance. There are others, too, too numerous to mention in my one chapter, but really we have a good circle of friends, and I no longer think with regret of Wilton. However, it is only one of the new circle of friends who impels her to these unwonted extravagances.

160

With regard to the horse she bought from her aunt, I am amazed to read the lessons go well. She grits her teeth each morning and puts on the riding habit with the gaping neck — really I think I must alter it, it bothers me so — and goes out for an hour, but when I peer out the window, I see her sitting as taut as a wire on the animal's back and am convinced those sudden starts the animal takes with her ears pulled back have not Priscilla's approval. She should be a good rider, for she was always athletic, but she wants a tamer mount to begin. She would have got one before now if Burne did not continue to tease her about it, and ask her if she has been thrown yet every time he comes. She would ride it now if it were a tiger, to show him she can do it. I have occasionally hinted that mulishness is an unlikely way to nab a husband, but she tells me I had better change, then, or Clavering will escape my clutches.

The recital of the grate episode is substantially correct. I do feel, however, that the voices I heard from the chimney were given short shrift. I described to her in some detail that they were voices — human or ghostly voices — not creaking timbers or any mechanical thing. They came from a throat I am convinced, but that it was a living throat I could not swear. There was an eerie, supernatural sound to them, possibly caused by the echoing effect of the chimney. I do not strongly believe in ghosts, but a phenomenon that recurs throughout history and in all parts of the world cannot be rejected out of hand only because it is not understood. In fact, my own mother, whom I mentioned having vivid recollections of the earthquake of 1750, claimed to have seen an apparition on the grounds of Longleat in 1775, when the lord and lady of the manor had graciously opened the park for a church garden fête. Other than the grate, I have had no personal contact with the supernatural. While we are on the subject of my mother, I shall clear up a little point that might have mystified you. It has been said I am a "connection" of the late Mr Denver and left at that. There is no mystery in my origins; I am not illegitimate or anything so raffish. My sister Wilma married Mr Denver's first cousin, Ivan Sinclair. That is the connection.

No doubt other things will occur to me after I have left off writing. I know I showed hackle every time my name cropped up in the story, as it *finally* did at the end of chapter one. Ah, yes, the shawl, the mustard shawl (to say nothing of the *ominous*-coloured mauve). There was a gratuitous insult. It is three-and-a-half years old, not five, and was plenty good enough until the Duke came into our lives. But you see who it is that is out to impress him. To finish off and bring it up to the present, I read that Clavering "often" came at night to read books with me. He came every single night that week, and also stopped in two afternoons on his way home from Anderida, and there was precious little book reading done, I can tell you. He frequently invited Priscilla out with him as well, but she stubbornly refused to go, for what reason I cannot fathom. He had the clavichord tuned and sent down immediately, the very next day, and often asked us to play for him in the evenings. He also brought her a box of dates (which he had sent down all the way from Londinium, I think, since there were none available in town), after I mentioned her liking them. He said they were the only thing he had heard of her liking, outside of wild nags that she couldn't handle, and she already had that. I write with embarrassment (for her behaviour reflects somewhat on my association with her) that she neither ate one nor even opened the package till he had gone. He was trying to court her, you see, but would have had better luck making up to a cabbage. I occasionally left them alone for brief periods, and always noticed when I returned that Burne had availed himself of a seat closer to her than when I had left, and on one occasion she was blushing, but I did not enquire what had passed, and naturally she did not tell me, I noticed that from that evening on she reverted to her yellow gown, so concluded he had complimented her on the green silk.

It remains only to straighten out the birthday gift from Clavering. I did not feign interest in it, nor was it a worthless, broken bit of rubbish, as you might be forgiven for concluding. It was purchased by a great uncle of his on a trip to Italy some years previously. It was primitive, which is to say not one of the large, classical copies of Greek work, but a bit of genuine Roman artwork, about fifteen inches high, very naturalistic, and there is no doubt as to the sex of the person in my mind. It is a small boy, holding a bunch of cherries, of which only one remains, but the statue itself is in perfect repair other than that. Its appropriateness rests in the cherry, of course, and I must say I think

Priscilla is particularly petty with regard to our mutual taste for the fruit. It has come to the point I hesitate to offer the man one, which is ludicrous with the quantity of them now in the house, for she bought another tin when she got the rose satin material. There, the dinner bell is sounding now, and I shall finish up.

Evening

I see Miss Slack has availed herself of my story without bothering to ask my approval. I have read over her account and can say only, "Balderdash!" However, in case I have inadvertently biased my account, I shall leave it in. She is quite correct to be angry at my neglecting to mention her name is Maude. Clavering did not come tonight, and we are both retiring early, since he has developed the rude habit of staying long past our first yawns, till midnight, in fact, and as we continue arising early, we are both fagged with his interminable visits.

CHAPTER
ELEVEN

I spent the next day in my sickbed where I was resting not because of a sudden onslaught of illness but because of a long overdue spill from Juliette. On Monday the day was fine — the whole autumn had been beautiful with more sun than we ever got at Wiltshire, and in the afternoon I decided to ride alone. I had had a lesson with George in the morning and had planned to go to Pevensey with Slack later, but she had to dash to Belview to borrow yet another book — his library shelves must be nearly empty — and so my rose gown remained at Miss Savage's shop, and it was to be finished that day. There was no immediate need of it after the spill, so it hardly mattered.

I became bored with the garden and decided to canter through Clavering's spinney. It is closer than my aunt's fields. She had dropped the hint she disliked a great deal of traffic in the park, since she was trying to grow some decent lawns there. I had permission to use the trap-free spinney, and intended doing no more than running through it once or twice on the footpath; but it happened that a stupid hare, of which there are many on Clavering's property due to his having killed his foxes, dashed across our path, and what should Juliette do but take a fright and break into one of her wild gallops. I was first only frightened, thinking I could control her, since she has occasionally pulled this trick on me before. On this occasion I did not succeed. When she got to the end of the spinney, she went mad with the vast expanse of meadow that suddenly opened up before her, and went galloping off into that trap infested area at a hair-raising speed. It was the fear of traps that made me panic. I envisioned one opening its maw and snapping on to her legs, myself being thrown wildly and breaking my head or a leg, or falling into another trap. I thought of them as being littered every few yards, but this was not true. We didn't see one during our whole gallop.

There soon arose before us a few remains of gray walls, the ruined chapel of Belview. I knew this to be the area particularly heavily trapped, and felt that if we were to be caught, this was where it would happen. I recount this now in a rational manner, but at the time I was irrational with fear, and hardly knew what I was seeing. I did catch, out of the corner of my eye, the sight of two men talking, and saw they had mounts standing by. Remembering the men who were to clear out the excavation for rebuilding, I assumed it was these workmen and shouted to them for help. The larger jumped on to a black stallion and came after me. The other also ran to his mount, but it was further away and it was the first whom I had some hopes would rescue me. I soon heard him clattering behind me, gaining on me in spite of Juliette's heart-pounding speed. He was soon at my side and reaching out one strong arm. I understood, quite naturally, I think, that I was meant to throw myself on to his arm, not that he could actually catch me, but it would break my fall. I summoned my wits and my courage and threw myself from Juliette's back. It was an error. What the man was doing was trying to snatch the reins and bring the horse to a stop. His arm moved beyond my grasp as I leapt, and I went falling perilously into a maelstrom of flying hooves and heaving flanks. There was very little time to consider it, a second or two, but in retrospect I realize I faced death. That was what accounted for my subsequent state of shock. A hoof on the temple might well have killed me — or made me a senseless mass for the rest of my life, which would have been infinitely worse. In a split-second I was on the ground, waiting for the inevitable stab of pain, for my head to fall open, for some excruciating agony in back or limb, presaging a life as a hopeless cripple. Miraculously, I felt only some slight discomfort in my left hip, which had taken the brunt of the fall. I heard more hooves coming from behind, the second man who had been there at the ruined chapel. He dismounted quickly and was at my side, while dimly the other set of hooves were heard to go further away, off into the distance. I was alive; I was well but was seized with a spasm of trembling at the shock of the ordeal, and could not speak. The man beside me was feeling gingerly with his fingers in my hair, my scalp, for blood or bumps, lifting my arms, feeling my body. I could hear him breathe rapidly and heavily, but he said nothing. I tried to open my lips to speak, and became unconscious. When I revived, I was

167

being carried off somewhere. I knew not where, nor did I care. Nothing hurt. It was warm and peaceful and safe being carried along. Someone was looking after me; it was all that mattered. I was a little annoyed when I again heard horses approaching from behind us.

"Go to the house and get the gig," the man carrying me said. It was a familiar voice. I was sure I had heard it before, but it sounded strained now, as though it came from a distance.

"What about the horses?" the other man asked. I had not heard that voice before. It was deep, rough.

"Take them home. All of them, especially that damned mare of Inglewood's."

"Aye, aye, sir," the second voice replied. He must be a sailor, I thought.

"And Lou — better send the gig with a groom. She might not have recognized you. I'll meet you later."

"Where are you taking her?" the sailor asked.

"I'll wait at the ruins."

"Righto." I heard the sound of harnesses jingling, and then the clop of horses leaving. I was very glad the interruption was over and I could go to sleep.

Some time later I had been laid down on a strip of grass, but not on the ground. There was a wall behind me, and the clear blue sky above. I was on a ledge with a grass surface, some feature of the ruined chapel. There was a coat tucked around me, inhibiting the arms. I turned my head to the right and saw Clavering glowering over me with a face that would have curdled cream. "You damned fool," he said harshly.

168

It seemed inordinately cruel that he should swear at me when I was so tired. I didn't even feel angry at this treatment. I was too tired. I closed my eyes again.

"Priscilla! Prissie, are you all right?" he demanded.

Let him worry, I thought and lay comfortably back, unresponsive. But I was not to be allowed my hard-earned rest. "Speak to me," he said angrily. The coat was ripped off, and my hands, ice-cold, were being chaffed. "It serves you right. I've told you a dozen times . . ." he went on in a fierce voice, then stopped and I felt a jerk as he turned around. "What in hell's keeping him?"

I was infinitely tired. I thought I might sleep forever but felt my eyelids flutter open of their own volition, and still that grim, angry face swam before me, not ten inches away.

"Do you recognize me?" he asked.

I frowned, not at the difficulty of the question, but at the pointlessness of it. How should I not know him, when he had been all but living at my house the past week? "Kn-know you?" I asked, intending irony, but hearing a weak, infant's puling voice issue from my lips.

"It's Clavering," he said, in a hard, taut voice.

I tried to lift my lids, but they weighed a ton each and were too heavy for my weakened condition.

"Damn your eyes, you're not going to die on me," he growled, and lifted my poor tired head from the grass. "Look at me!"

I was much inclined to obey to silence him, but could not.

169

"Priscilla, speak to me! Say *something!*" he commanded sternly. The loud voice hurt my head. "Be quiet," I managed to get out, very weakly.

"You'll live," he said, and laughed, also weakly, then returned my head to its resting place.

I felt the coat being tucked around my arms again. With a very uncomfortable rustling about, Clavering sat down at my head, and then lifted it to ease his lap under me. He made a very poor pillow, and my peace was further disturbed by having his large, cold hand pass over my cheeks and through my hair, while a continuous stream of vicious blandishments were poured over me.

"It serves you right. I have repeatedly told you you couldn't handle that damned nag. You're lucky she didn't trample you. I hope you've learned your lesson once and for all. Damn that lackey! What's taking him so long?" Then in a tone only a shade softer. "Does it hurt anywhere, Priss? Are you in pain? We'll soon have you home. Where is that gig? Dear God, we must be waiting half an hour!" That was the nature of his soothing comfort. Abuse, liberally interspersed with profanity and curses on me and his servants.

Finally the unfortunate person chosen for the chore arrived. "Where's the blanket?" Clavering demanded, arising quickly, but not quite throwing my head to the grass.

There was an apologetic muttering on the absence of a blanket, followed by a fresh string of curses sworn off on the stupidity of servants. "Pass the brandy. She's as white as snow." More apologetic mutterings. "Well,

170

there's some in the . . . Oh, hell, never mind. Help me lift her. Take her feet. Gently, she's not a side of beef."

I felt very like one by the time I was stowed in the dog cart, or whatever the vehicle it was that the servant had chosen to negotiate the rough ride through the meadows. Clavering managed the single horse with one hand and held me on to the seat beside him with the other, for I was partially revived and could sit up. In fact, I was feeling better even without brandy and was already beginning to form a few questions in my mind, but was not yet stout enough to give them voice. We joggled through the meadow, into the spinney, where branches of bushes brushed against our sides. Clavering had no hand free to fend them off, nor had I, bound as I was in his coat, with the arms tucked in behind me. Letting go of my waist, he pushed my face quite roughly into his shoulder, asking if I hadn't the sense to duck my head when it was being lashed with thorns, which was, of course, a gross exaggeration. There were a few harmless leaves touching my hair, no more.

I believe it was his intention to carry me bodily into Willow Hall from the stables, but I was sufficiently myself by that time that I forbade such nonsense. I shrugged myself out of his jacket and suggested he put it on before he contracted lung fever, if he hadn't already. He returned it to my shoulders and did up two buttons, with my arms clamped to my sides beneath it, then put his arm around my back, and as he had arms like an ape, there was sufficient length left over for him also to hold my waist. In this extremely uncomfortable manner we negotiated the few yards to the kitchen door, which he entered bellowing for Slack.

"Be quiet! You'll scare her out of her wits," I said sharply.

"That's twice today you've hushed me. Fine thanks for saving your life."

"It was the other man who saved my life, and very awkwardly he did it, too."

"I'm happy to see you're returning to normal," he said, then hollered, "Slack!" again, very loudly. Slack, not Maude, by the way.

She came hot-foot from her books, and looked closer to fainting than I was myself. She insisted in adding to my discomfort by grabbing my other side, but despite them I made it to the saloon and the sofa.

"The doctor! We must call the doctor at once!" she babbled.

"I don't need a doctor."

"Call him," Clavering decreed. "And get some wine."

She darted off, returning with the wine bottle and no glass. Poor Slack was very upset. Clavering tipped the bottle to my lips. My initial idea of clenching my lips was abandoned when I foresaw the likelihood of having liquid drooling down my chin like an infant or senile invalid. He tipped my head back and a great cascade of wine, too much for my mouth to hold, flowed forth, down my chin, and over my riding habit, bringing me to spluttering rigidity in an upright position.

"Get away before you drown me. I'm not hurt, and I don't want a doctor, either. Give me your handkerchief."

"You remembered not to say please. You must be recovering," he said, and pulled out a handkerchief, to dab at my chin, but as my bosom was also well doused, he handed it to me. No sooner had I daubed up the excess, lamenting the ruin of my jacket, than I was summarily pushed back against the pillows.

"Your turn to be quiet." He looked about the room for a blanket and, finding none, grabbed Slack's grey-purple shawl to throw over me.

"I am not in the least cold. I'm hot," I said, pushing it away.

"You are suffering from shock. Wine and warmth are the treatment," he said, putting the shawl back on, and lifting the bottle again.

"Would it be possible to have a glass, if you insist on forcing wine down my throat?"

"No. Drink it," he ordered, and held the bottle again, but I had the wits to steady it myself this time, and got a mouthful without spilling the rest of the bottle. It was then I noticed his hand shaking. It was trembling like a leaf in the wind.

"What's the matter with you?" I asked. "Have you got the trembles? You've been drinking too much."

"I haven't been drinking enough," he replied, and took the remainder of the bottle for himself, still without a glass.

Slack returned to find him at this genteel pastime, and ran off for a goblet, leaving him free to continue the sermon of my amazing display of stubbornness in insisting on trying to ride Juliette. "I have told you a dozen times . . ." he began.

"No, Your Grace, you have told me *at least* a hundred times, and I am mighty tired of hearing it. I had not the skill to handle her. I shouldn't have persisted against your omniscient warnings. *Mea culpa, mea culpa, mea maxima culpa,* and Amen."

"You're not to try it again."

"Never again. I'll give her back to Lady Inglewood, and may she break her head as she nearly did mine. Yes, it would serve me well if I had. Sorry to disappoint you. But if your clumsy friend had helped me instead of moving his arm just as I thought he was going to catch me . . ."

"He did exactly the right thing. He would have had her stopped in a minute. He nearly had his hands on the reins. Why you took it into your empty head to throw yourself off a runaway animal in full gallop when you had managed to hold on to your seat that long is beyond me. Next time . . ."

"There isn't going to be a next time. I have heeded your dozens of warnings."

Slack came back with the glasses just as the bottle was emptied, and was scurrying off for another bottle, but Clavering called her back. "Tell me what happened," she said to him, and he proceeded to give her a highly coloured and totally inaccurate account of my mishap.

"I knew it! I have told her a dozen times . . ." Slack began to tell him.

I sighed, defeated, and closed my eyes. They decided it was rest the invalid now required, and fell silent. I heard a chair being brought to the edge of the sofa and someone sat down. When I felt my cover being straightened and the hair brushed from my forehead, I assumed it was Slack and reached out for her hand. But, of course, when I felt a hairy paw I realized my error.

"Too late," he said, as I tried to jerk away, and he held on to it tightly.

I looked around the room for Slack, but she had deserted us. "She's gone to see to boiling water," he told me.

"I'm not having a baby," I pointed out.

"I'm glad to hear it," was his unfeeling reply.

I should have had an answer but was suddenly too tired. I was dizzy from the fall and perhaps the wine, gulped down in haste. I think I slept, or rested anyway. Later Slack came in and told me the doctor was delayed, but would come around after dinner.

"That is totally unnecessary," I told her, and sat up. Finding no reeling in my head, I put my feet on the floor and pushed aside the shawl.

"Are you hungry?" Slack asked. "It's nearly dinner-time, but I didn't have the table laid."

"No, I'm not hungry."

"You have something, Maude," Clavering told her. "I'll stay with Priss. Better for her not to eat till the doctor comes."

"Would you like a plate?" she asked him.

"Later."

She left, the idea being that they would take shifts minding me, as if I were an unruly child or wayward moonling.

175

"How did you come to be there, at the chapel with that man?" I asked. I had been thinking about this and other things ever since the trip home in the dog cart.

"I am having it shored up, the loose stones mortared into place for safety's sake."

"Lazy Louie isn't a stone mason. He's a smuggler."

"That wasn't Lazy Louie."

"Yes, it was. I've seen him on that big black stallion before, and you called him Louie, too."

"How do you come to know an unsavoury character like that?"

"I don't know him, except by sight, but *you* seem to be on much better terms with him. What was he doing there?"

"I told you. His uncle from Hythe does that sort of work, and Louie is going to get him to come to me. He was looking it over for his uncle, to give him an idea of the nature of the job."

"Why did you say it wasn't he?"

"I was afraid you'd take into your head to go thanking him the next time you see him, and he is not the sort of fellow you ought to be talking to."

"Eel! Officer Smith says Louie is one, and you're another. You didn't want me to see him. You said — Oh, I can't remember. Why can't I remember? You said for him to go away, because maybe I hadn't seen him. What are you up to, Clavering?"

"Rescuing maidens in distress, and being given a hard time for it."

"And there was brandy, too."

"Louie always reeks of brandy. An occupational hazard."

"No, I don't mean I smelled it. You said something. You asked the groom for brandy. What would you be doing with brandy at Belview? You shouldn't buy smuggled brandy."

"I don't. Someone gave me a bottle, which I keep for medicinal purposes."

"And when he hadn't brought it, you said there was some — somewhere else . . ."

"You were dreaming. I said nothing of the sort. You were supposed to be unconscious. Why were you frightening the life out of me if you were wide awake the whole time?"

"I wasn't wide awake, worse luck. Only half."

He didn't say a word, but I noticed his eyes flickering to the grate in a worried way.

"Burne, what is it about?" I asked, hoping to entice him to tell me by using a dulcet tone and his preferred name, for it was becoming plain that something strange was afoot.

"What do you mean?" he asked, unseduced by either tone or name.

"I mean your meeting with that man, and having brandy, and lying about it. I mean men disappearing in your meadow, and your talk of building a Roman temple when there aren't enough stones there to build a decent-sized dog kennel. And certainly not enough stone to protect with mantraps. And another thing, why is it I never fall into a trap in that meadow? That's twice now I've been there, and never a sign of a trap."

"I'll see if I can't arrange to place one in your way next time you go sniffing about."

"That's not an answer."

"Actually it's not the few stones I want to protect; it's the Roman foundation under those few stones above-ground. There's a piece of mosaic floor in fairly good condition for one thing."

"That doesn't explain anything."

"What are you suggesting?" he asked. "That I lie in wait in the tall grass, to kidnap any hapless victims who trespass? Kill them and dispose of the bodies? That I am in league with Lazy Louie smuggling brandy from France? Would you like a keg?" he asked in a conspiratorial voice.

"No, but I don't doubt you could arrange it if I did. For medicinal purposes, of course."

"Anyone in the village could arrange it. Your friend McMaster would be happy to help you. My views on the matter are pretty generally known, and *I* might have a little more trouble than others."

"I wasn't accusing you of *smuggling*, Clavering. On that point at least you are above suspicion. Is there buried treasure in the meadow — is that it?"

"Yes, a priceless Roman mosaic. What idiotic notion have you hatched now, Prissie?"

It did sound rather idiotic all of a sudden, and I rapidly changed to another point of some little mystery. "You said a long time ago, when you asked us to Belview, that you would be going back to London very soon, to Parliament. What keeps you on here?"

"Do you really have to ask?"

"Don't try to pretend it's me and Slack."

"Slack has nothing to do with it, but don't, pray, tell her I have been leading her on."

"Neither have I anything to do with it. And you haven't raised your offer for Seaview for *weeks*, either."

"I have thought of a cheaper way to get it."

"I knew that was what you were up to! I told Slack so."

"Did you indeed? That was a little previous of you."

"What do you mean? You've been trying to deceive us that you're our friend, lending us the clavichord and so on, so that we'll be beholden to you. Giving Slack the run of your library . . ."

"Well, upon my word! I knew you were the most stubborn woman God ever created, but this is the first time I ever realized the extent of your conniving, scheming brain — and laying the whole of it in *my* dish, if you please! It would not have occurred to me to *manipulate* you in that under-handed way. My scheming, if it even merits the word after what you have thought — is quite open and aboveboard."

"Except for the part of it that takes place underground with Roman mosaics, or in secluded meadows with smugglers. Never mind. We'll argue tomorrow. My head aches."

"I won't be here tomorrow."

"You're not leaving!"

He smiled softly and took my hand. "Do you know, I think that is the first nice thing you've ever said to me, and the strain of uttering it has given you a migraine. I will be back soon."

"What was nice about it?" I asked, for I had certainly intended no compliment.

"The anxious tone, Priss. Very nice."

"I was not anxious."

"You don't have to apologize. *Au contraire.*"

There was no point in arguing with him, and besides, my head did ache. Slack must have gobbled her dinner. She was back within minutes, carrying a tray for Clavering, from which he ate at a table in the room. The first meal he had ever taken with us, and what a ramshackle meal it was, sitting alone at a deal table in a corner. He remained till the doctor came, not so much later. After a brief examination, the doctor left a quite unnecessary sleeping draught, which I never did take, but which Slack kept for an emergency. As soon as Doctor Sloane was gone, Clavering, too, arose to take his leave. Slack, with some misguided idea of tact, decided to leave us alone, for which I upbraided her severely later.

Privacy was not in the least necessary for our last words. "Recover quickly," was his parting solicitude, delivered in his customary curt, commanding way.

"I am recovered."

"And stay out of the meadow. Louie's uncle might be there. He's as bad as his nephew — worse, a drunkard and renowned womanizer."

"You entrust your priceless Roman mosaic to a drunkard? You amaze me, Your Grace."

"He has orders to be sobered up, and when he is, he's the best worker in the country."

"Eel!"

180

"Time for me to join the eelfare. Pity, I would like very much to stay and wrestle with you — verbally, of course. Recuperate!" he ordered, punctuating his command with a pointing finger; then he turned and left the room.

I overheard him talking to Slack in the hall. "Take care of her," he said. "I'll be back as soon as I can."

As Slack made no startled exclamation, I assumed she had been told before of his leaving. "I'll keep Juliette at Belview till I return. I wouldn't put it past her to try the wretch again to spite me."

Luckily for Slack, I couldn't make out her answer, but I heard that eel laughing. "But that is exactly what I like about her," he said. "Birds of a feather, we two." Then the outer door closed, and Slack came back to me, looking suspiciously innocent. I'd have given another diamond ring to know what she had said, but would not satisfy her to ask.

I was given a light supper a little later on, then went early to bed because of my headache. Slack, in a fit of guilt, cleaned up my riding habit, and now that I had not the least intention of ever donning it again, also took pity on my poor stitchery and fixed up the gaping neck. I don't believe she can have read a single chapter of her books that evening.

CHAPTER
TWELVE

I recovered quickly from the accident. Already the next day I was up and about the house, but was content to remain indoors, since the weather was inclement. Lady Inglewood and George came to call, which is the only reason I bothered having a relapse in the afternoon. Slack told them the story, and Lady Inglewood, after expressing every concern, offered to buy back Juliette. I expect she was missing her rides. With nothing better to do, I glanced through a few of the many books Slack had borrowed from Clavering. One dealt with the Forts of the Saxon Shore, and I was interested to learn that there was the remains of one at Pevensey. Also curious, since they were not normally spaced so close together as to allow of another at Willow Hall, only three miles away. There was a much greater distance between the others, at Lympne, Richborough, Pevensey, and Portsmouth. In fact, I realized at once that it was unlikely in the extreme that what we were built on was an old fort at all; it must be some other Roman ruin. I looked through other books, trying to discover what might be the foundation of my home, but there was a deal too much to make any decision.

They erected temples, villas, stores, forums, baths, and garrisons with a prolificity that was truly astounding. Their engineering feats, too, were impressive. Central heating, for instance, was common and a luxury not indulged in in our own modern times to any extent. Their skill in transporting water, clearing swamps and filling them in for building purposes, erecting bridges, building foundations and piers under water, and building roads sixteen to twenty-four feet wide of metalled surfaces was surely unparalleled in their time, and hardly surpassed since. Pleased that I was showing any interest in her hobby, Slack surrounded me with a wall of books dealing with their art, trade, politics, and religion. Had I had the time or interest to read half of them, I would have been an expert, but I had not the least intention of sharing her mania.

I did continue to wonder though about the ruins under Seaview. A fort at Pevensey indicated a military establishment hereabouts, and if the ruined chapel in the meadow was built on a Roman temple as Clavering had indicated, there was more than military goings-on in the area. A settlement. It might be built on a villa, or even a bath. The diagrams outlining the arrangement of the baths were impressive and interesting. Huge things, allowing a thousand or more to bathe at one time, and quite a ritual they made of it, with athletics first and oiling their bodies afterward. I could not suppress a twinge to think of taking a bath in the presence of nine hundred and ninety-nine other persons, but at least they had running water, and separate hours for women and men.

On the second day I drove into Pevensey to fetch my rose satin gown, with a little misgiving as to what Slack would say when she observed the daring neckline and lack of sleeves. I looked about sharply for Lazy Louie, for whatever Clavering had to say on the subject, I felt I owed him my thanks. He was not to be seen anywhere, and later Officer Smith, of whom I enquired at the Customs Office, told me the *Nancy-Jane* had slipped away a day ago, and he would keep an eye peeled for its return. I also enquired of Lazy Louie's last name, for I seemed to remember Smith's having mentioned it once, and I thought I ought to address him as Mr Something when I met him.

"He's a FitzHugh," Smith said, with a sly smile that told me there was some significance in the name. A question caused him to elaborate.

"One of old Lord Hugh's by-blows."

"Who is Lord Hugh?" I asked. It was not unlike trying to extract information from George.

"Why, he was uncle to the Duke of Clavering, the father's younger brother. Long since buried, but the countryside hereabouts bears many a trace of him, if you know what I mean," he said roguishly. "He did better for most of them than he did for Louie, but the lad was a renegade from the beginning, and there was no making him respectable. It does bother His Grace no end that the lad has turned bad; it's why he is so determined to catch him. Clavering has tried his hand more than once to reform the fellow; set him up as a horse breeder, but all he ever got for that is the stallion he rides. There was some falling out between them. They don't hardly nod when they pass on the street."

I was hard-pressed not to break into whoops of laughter in the man's face. The illustrious Duke of Clavering, half a cousin to Lazy Louie, that "unsavoury character" too low for me to speak to. A smuggler, a bastard, and a renegade. How I would crow when next we met! There was no reason to doubt Smith's story. I had even thought I glimpsed some small similarity between them, and it was true they both rode huge black stallions. "It doesn't bother you then?" Smith asked, with an inquisitive face. The question left me speechless.

"Why should it bother me?" I asked.

He was taken aback, looked embarrassed, as though he had ventured to say more than he should have. I really think the man was intimating there was something between Clavering and me, and he was in need of a setting down. "It does bother me a little that you can't seem to catch the one smuggler you have to deal with. But you know he is out, and surely won't let him land a load *again*."

Till I was out of his office, I held in my secret delight. This discovery was of more worth to me than my new rose satin gown, which I think might warrant a warmer description than being "dressed up a little." Not that I had any place to wear such a dashing ensemble, unless someone should decide to hold a ball. For the next few days there was no ball, nor any excitement of any sort save a visit from Mr McMaster.

With my rides discontinued, George was coming to find our visits as dull as I always had myself. He had no excuse now to talk horses, and curtailed his calls to a very agreeable twenty minutes. Lady Inglewood came once to see what she could find out about our dealings with Clavering, and was so vexed to see his clavichord in my saloon that she didn't return. His being safely away in London may have lessened her vigilance, and in any case from Wednesday on we saw no sign of her.

With so little to do in my convalescence, I turned to books, like Slack, and read of the glories of Roman Britain. I was curious to see examples of the mosaic floors and muralled walls that once graced the homes of the mighty, but most of all I envied them their central heating, ingeniously contrived by conduits in walls. and floors. The heat was made by coal, surface-mined, I read. Why could we not install it nowadays? I found it wonderful that some roads remained when they had built five thousand miles of them. Again and again I returned to puzzle the mystery of what ancient building once stood where today Seaview, or Willow Hall, now stands. With Clavering away, I felt less intense about the name of my house somehow. He did not write to us, of course. We did not expect that he would do so. He would be busy in Parliament, where the war against Napoleon must surely be one of the major matters for discussion. He had not said exactly when he would return. *Soon* is a relative term — it might be a week or a month, but with London only sixty miles away I didn't think a trip in Clavering's well-sprung carriage need wait a month.

The war dragged on. Since Wellington's victory at Vittoria in June, he had been advancing on the French frontier. It was hoped he would soon be in France. And with Napoleon's army weakened from the Russian battles, and with the Prussian War of Liberation using what men and guns he had left, we were hopeful of a victory at last. I did not really fear invasion; it was not spoken of locally as being at all a likely thing. Still, with Napoleon, one could never be sure. England's armies, too, were largely dispersed elsewhere, and the possibility could never be ignored entirely. The round Martello Towers were a welcome safeguard, but a reminder, as well.

I became impatient with our dull routine. Slack did nothing to soothe my exacerbated nerves. Coy remarks that I was "lonely" and that we might take a jaunt up to Londinium were treated with the contempt they deserved, but we did make some halfhearted plans for visiting Brighton the next summer, a stylish resort and close to us. This sent Slack dashing up to Belview to see what she could discover of its older name, and what she might find of interest to an historian like herself. I informed her that what I intended to see was the Prince Regent's pavilion, and I doubted very much if even her precious Romans had ever done anything to outshine it in opulence, extravagance, and folly. I also wondered if it had central heating. But, of course, an onion dome and Chinese decor held no interest for her. She learned at Belview that the Duke was expected home "soon," and got it pinned down a little more firmly than I what his "soon" meant.

"Tomorrow or the day after; before the next week definitely. They say he's never away above a week," she said.

While Slack was gone, I decided to take a walk, and chose to walk through Clavering's spinney, the same through which I had permission to ride; I could not feel walking would be prohibited. As I approached the far end of it, I went just a distance into the meadow, to see if there was any sign of Louie's uncle, (maternal, I presume) working on the ruins. I was careful of traps, looking with a sharp eye before every footstep. I could see in the distance one mount, a dappled grey which I did not recognize, nor did I see any sign of its rider. There was no work going on. The ruins stood in a flat field, and scaffolds or piles of equipment or mortar or cement must have been visible had they been there. It seemed the uncle like the nephew was indeed a brandy lover, and was probably asleep in the ruins. Being a little frightened of both traps and drunken stone-masons, I turned my steps around and went back home.

A rather vicious storm blew up that night. Already at dinnertime it was dark and cool. We lit the fire in the grate and settled in for a comfortable evening with our books. The grate had been silent as a mouse for some time now, and we had become complacent about it, but at nine o'clock it began to tremble a little, and we exchanged silent expressions of chagrin.

It rattled again, and Slack said, "Not that business again," voicing my sentiments exactly. We set our jaws for trouble, but there was actually little enough to complain of — a few minor jiggles that might well have been caused by the howling winds outside.

"Burne couldn't come tonight if he wanted to," Slack commented. "Home from Londinium, I mean."

"Missing him, are you?" I quizzed her. "Go ahead and eat your cherries without him, Slack. It will make you feel closer to him."

"Oh, I feel close enough just reading his books," she answered quietly, inured to my taunts.

I had, of course, told her the moment I returned from Pevensey some days previously about Clavering's relationship to Lazy Louie. Without knowing a single thing about it, she denied all kinship. Then went on to explain it away as a harmless thing anyway, if Burne's uncle should have been a rakeshame, and she was sure there were more Fitzes in England than FitzHughs. Furthermore, Lazy Louie bore not the slightest trace of resemblance to Burne, and what if they did both have black eyes? For that matter, she personally hadn't a thing against smuggling, and neither did I, apparently, for I bought up every scrap of silk the drapery shop had for sale, yards and yards of it, in all shades of the rainbow.

"Clavering's cousin won't be coming home tonight, either," I said.

"You refer to Lazy Louie, his *alleged* half-cousin, do you?"

"Yes, the bastard-smuggler of the family."

"Such talk is not becoming in a lady, Priscilla, and I'm sure I don't know what Burne would say if you carry on so."

"Neither do I, but I'm dying to find out."

"Well, he's right about you is all I can say," she retorted sharply.

"What did he say?" I asked, ready to take umbrage.

She sniffed and snorted for a few moments, but eventually I got it out of her. "He said you were always fixing for a fight with him, and so you are."

"Did he, indeed? Gallant of him!"

"And he's not much better if it comes to that. Birds of a feather."

That is exactly what I like about her. Oh yes, he'd hear my views on Lazy Louie all right. Slack knew there was no point trying to talk me out of it, and suggested a little music instead. We had played our few standard pieces to death, and I thought I had seen some music books in the bottom of the parson's bench; so we opened it and pulled piles of magazines out on to the floor to search through them. But they were so ancient as to be unknown even to Slack, and neither of us is such a fine musician that she does a good job of timing a piece with which she is unfamiliar, so it was not a great success.

"I'm for bed," Slack said after a short musical interlude. "I feel a touch of the headache. Not that I'll sleep with that storm going on outside. I'll just tidy up that welter of books and close the parson's bench."

"That is why we have servants, Slack," I told her, and convinced her to leave it to Sally, for she was holding her head, and this indicated one of her bad headaches, which come to trouble her once or twice a year. "Why don't you take a few drops of that sleeping draught the doctor left for me? It will give you a good night's sleep."

"I think perhaps I will. A good thing I didn't throw it away."

We both went up to bed early, but as we had been doing so all week, I was not at all tired. I lit a brace of candles and read till close to midnight, and was still not sleepy. Even after I blew out the candles and lay for some three-quarters of an hour, sleep did not come. I became quite vexed with myself. The longer I lay there, staring fixedly into the darkness, the less did I feel like sleeping. My mind roamed over all the past weeks since coming to Seaview, and as I reviewed it, it seemed people had been trying to push me into doing things I had no desire to do since the moment I had arrived. First Lady Inglewood trying to push me into marrying George, then Clavering trying to make me sell him Seaview, Slack trying to make me into a lover of antiquity, and even myself, making me ride a horse I despised. And now trying to sleep when it was perfectly obvious my body was saturated with sleep. I would get up and do something. No matter if the clock was approaching one. I could stay in bed as long as I chose tomorrow. And I wouldn't bother reading about any more Roman ingenuity, either. I would find myself a good, romantic novel and indulge in a bout of emotion. Between the storm and my old Gothic mansion, I was in a mood for Mrs Radcliffe tonight, and regretted my old friend had remained behind as a gift to the circulating library at Wilton. There was no proper library at Seaview, but in the morning parlour there were a few bookshelves built in under the window, and I remembered seeing the tell-tale marble-covered books denoting the Minerva Press. I lit my candelabrum and slipped into my dressing-gown and houseslippers to go down to the morning parlour. My saloon is to the right of the staircase as one descends, and I took a peek in to see if the embers had burned themselves out so that I might close the flue, for it was still raining, but more gently now.

I neither heard nor suspected a thing amiss till I took up the poker to stir the embers, now cold. Then I heard it, the old familiar rattling of the grate. Not loud, but definite, and it was no fire nor howling wind that caused it. Certainly nothing but a human voice that produced that echoing laugh. My hair did not stand on end, but it lifted. I could feel a strange prickling sensation on my scalp, feel it move along my neck and spine, right down to my toes. My arm, extended beyond its sleeve in reaching with the poker, was covered with gooseflesh. I stood frozen to the spot, with my ears stretched. It came again, quite distinctly audible in the silent, sleeping house — came, it seemed, from a different quarter. Glancing in its direction, I noticed we had left the lid of the parson's bench open after getting out our music, and strange and impossible as it was, the second burst of laughter came right out of the parson's bench. Naturally I hurried to it, looked in at an innocent varnished chest-bottom, with one magazine lying there.

I lifted out the magazine and examined the floor of the bench carefully. It had an indentation, a groove large enough for four fingers along the left end. My taper trembling in my left hand, I put my fingers of the right hand into the groove, and it lifted as silently and easily as though it were on oiled hinges, though in fact it was not attached at all. It was a loose piece of wood, varnished, and resting on a protruding frame-work beneath. Without a sound I took it out and laid it on the floor, and knelt down with the taper above my head to examine what was revealed below the now-bottomless bench. There was a pair of narrow steps leading into pitch blackness, and there was quite distinctly the sound of more than one voice coming in a muted fashion up from the blackness. I could see no more, but obviously there was something between the voices and me, a wall or a closed door. And equally obviously, the voices were coming from under the ground outside my Roman wall. They were in some excavation just outside the walls of my house. So I had found my secret passageway at last, right where Pickering thought it was. All the heavings at the bench had been unnecessary — the passage was right through it.

I sat back on my heels, breathing in light, fearful gasps. Who was it? The foolish thought of long-dead Roman centurions or soldiers gambling there flashed into my head. Ghosts of Caesar's legions, trapped inside their fort, which was not and never had been a fort. Why they should be gamboling their way through eternity I knew not, but there was a sound of merry-making, of laughter and happy voices, suggesting a party, with wine and possibly even women. No surly, sullen ghosts in any case. I was torn by the conflicting desires to dash upstairs to my room as fast as my legs could carry me, and to summon up my courage and descend the stair. I don't know how long I knelt there, but when I finally stood up the blood rushed through my legs, causing pins and needles to prick, and when I tried to take a step my feet were numb and cramped. The voices finally died out — in my mind I pictured legionnaires wearing metal armour and plumed helmets taking a ceremonial leave of each other. And still I stood on, craning my ears, imagining impossible scenes. I should call Slack and Wilkins, I thought when it became totally silent and my imagination had settled down. And what would I tell them? I heard ghosts laughing behind a closed door? For an eternity I stood thinking, listening, trying to decide what to do; then I remembered Slack had taken a sleeping draught, and really I could not like to go to Wilkins's door in the middle of the night in my dressing gown. It would have to wait till morning for a thorough investigation, but my curiosity would not let me leave without just taking a peek into the blackness. Whoever had been there was gone now — for a long time I had not heard a sound. I would venture down the stairs, just a little way to see if I could discover a door. Just a quick peek, and come right back up. There was definitely a barricade there. I would not be seen, even if there was someone still there.

I held my skirts up with one hand, my candelabrum in the other, rather wishing I had a third for the poker, and walked daintily down the narrow little staircase.

194

Before I was halfway down I saw a door. Just an ordinary door; it was even panelled, which gave a sense of security, ordinariness to the bizarre affair. It might have been a door into a bedroom or cheeseroom, and had quite plainly come from some such place. It looked so harmless, so completely innocent that I was emboldened to try the knob. A plain white porcelain knob, much as those abovestairs. I tried it. It turned half a revolution, then stopped. The door was locked, and still no sound came from beyond it, so whoever had been there had left, and it would be an ideal time to enter, if only the door weren't locked. Sufficient sense had returned to me that I no longer thought of Roman centurions, but English desperadoes of some kind. I rattled the knob harder, turned and rattled it several times, but it held. As I was about to turn and go back up the stairs, it pulled suddenly, noiselessly, into the black cavern beyond, and a short dark stranger with an evil face stood pointing a gun at my eyes.

He wore a black toque, dark and rough clothing. He was short, wiry, very strong looking. "*Entrez, ma'mselle,*" he said in a velvet, deep, calm voice, standing back, but always keeping his muzzle pointed at me.

A Frenchman! What on earth was one of Boney's men doing in my Roman fort? A Roman soldier would hardly have surprised me more. But this man was no soldier, nor was he a dream. He was very solid flesh and blood, and he did not mean to be disobeyed.

CHAPTER
THIRTEEN

I didn't say a word, or try to. Nor did I risk trying to scramble back up the stairs. I knew perfectly well the gun was loaded and didn't doubt for a minute he would use it. Neither did I accept his invitation to enter his parlour. I stood immobile, staring.

Quick as a lizard he had a steely hand on my wrist and was dragging me beyond the door, roughly and with determination. I opened my mouth to scream, to direct one desperate appeal up the stairway, and felt a hand clamped over my mouth, even as he kicked the door shut behind us. The candelabrum went hurtling to the floor, narrowly missing my skirt in the process. One taper remained burning, and with a flash of his black arm, the man had the one candle pulled out and held up to examine me.

"*Silence*," he decreed, in French, and using a voice I was not inclined to argue with. He took one step backward and slid a bolt on the door. It didn't make a sound, which accounted for my not having heard him slide it open a moment before; but this time he was sliding it shut, barricading me into a dark, dank room with him, this Frenchman with the wicked eyes. Curious as I was to examine the chamber, I couldn't tear my eyes from his face. I didn't dare. He no longer had a hand on me. He stood perhaps two feet away, looking, moving the candle up and down to allow a view of my face, and dressing-gown. This done in a bold and deliberate and leisurely way, he stood back and smiled. "*Charmante*," he decided.

Whatever I had feared prior to this — beating, being tied up, killed perhaps — my fears took a sudden jolt in a different direction. He looked lecherous, eyeing me hungrily.

"*Asseyez-vous, ma'mselle*," he said, and stepped back to reveal two barrels lined up against a stone wall. A certain odour emanated from them, a pungent smell — brandy, of course. The man was a smuggler. Odd it hadn't occurred to me sooner. It was his being French that had fooled me, but the two warring nations could always work in harness for criminal profit, and he must have English allies. I made no move to accept the proffered seat. I stood watching him, mesmerized like a moth by a flame, or a mouse by an attacking snake would be a more appropriate comparison.

While these discoveries were being made, already I was thinking of escape. The parson's bench — the lid was open. If anyone chanced into the saloon he would see it, come down the stairs. And be confronted with a locked door. Why had I not tried to rouse Slack, or called Wilkins? Too late. And no one would enter the saloon before morning. Oh, God — morning — *hours* away, while this black-eyed reptile devoured me.

"*Asseyez-vous, ma'mselle*," he repeated, more sharply now, the velvet beginning to scratch.

I thought it best to sit, and did so fearfully on the edge of the barrel nearer me. He immediately took up a seat on the other, making me realize it was closer than I liked.

"*Parlez-vous français?*" he asked, the voice calm again.

I had a nodding acquaintance with the language. "*Un peu,*" I answered, hearing the fear making my voice shake and trying to steady it.

"*Ah, bon! Vous êtes toute à fait charmante.*" A hand came out and stroked my cheek. I lifted my head quickly away, and the fingers took a hold of my chin, forcing it back. He looked into my frightened eyes and laughed, a deep, anticipatory chuckle.

"*Les anglaises,*" he said mockingly, almost caressingly.

A million thoughts jumbled through my poor brain. Fear was uppermost, fear of what would come next. Escape was not far behind it. To make a dash for the door to the stairway was the most simple means, but the delay of sliding the bolt would allow him time to catch me. He was agile, moving like quicksilver. He wouldn't be a split-second behind me. I next began to examine the room for other means of exit. He certainly hadn't entered by the door I had, and a different means of escape might be more practical.

The lone taper gave only a very weak illumination. I saw stone walls about, with one on the far side that looked to be of some other material, smoother, lighter; but of more interest, on my right, was a yawning black hole. Escape — but by what means? Was it a tunnel?

198

And if so, how long, and where did it exit? Would I meet the rest of the band if I tried that exit? It might lead directly to the sea, for there was a mystery as to how the men got brandy here without being seen by either Officer Smith or Clavering's patrol. Fear and indecision kept me where I was, and, of course, only a very short time had elapsed in any case, though to me it was an eternity. I half worried that other smugglers would come, and half wished they would, for there was something ominous in being alone with this amorous Frenchman. I recalled, too, the various tales I had heard about these "Gentlemen" — so wrongly named. Officer Smith had played down their ferocity, but still their little prank of pushing his head into a rabbit hole and pinning him there had never seemed very humourous to me, and with a woman I feared the treatment would be quite different — worse. Besides, this smuggler was French, and at the height of a war with France, I had heard many tales of the rapacity and viciousness of the French. Clavering had said they would be likely to single out two unprotected women. He had been right all along. The smugglers were using our doorstep for their activities, and I regretted Burne had not gone ahead with his excavation and found them out.

This brought to mind Lazy Louie, and I found myself wondering if I would have to deal with him, too, before the night was over. That "unsavoury character," there would be no help from him, though he had saved my life once. Oh, how I wished I had thanked him, had ingratiated myself. But to claim friendship with him might delay my fate, and I decided to try it. I cleared my throat nervously and began, ascribing to him his formal name.

"*Monsieur FitzHugh, Monsieur Louis FitzHugh est mon ami. Je le connais très bien,*" I said.

He threw his head back and laughed raucously. This gave him a very poor idea of my character, indeed, and before I knew what was happening, one black arm had shot out to encircle my waist and pull me to my feet. Simultaneously, I heard heavy footsteps approaching, and before long my good old friend Lazy Louie hunched through the yawning black hole that I had hoped would be my exit. I stared at him in horror. Like the Frenchman, he wore a black toque and dark clothing. He looked at us, struck dumb momentarily. I didn't know what to expect, but I knew that if that bull had in mind the same fate for me as his friend, I would rather be dead.

"Christ on a crutch, man!" Louie shouted, and rushed forward to pull the Frenchman away by violent force and push him quite unceremoniously against the wall.

"Are you all right, miss?" he asked, with horror glowing in his eyes. In that moment, I loved him. I felt like throwing myself against his massive chest and weeping, but years of self-control overcame my urge and I only drooped. He put out an arm to steady me; I didn't flinch, but grabbed it. This time his arm didn't fail me. It held firmly. "He didn't — didn't *molest* you, did he?" he asked fearfully.

The Frenchman entered into a string of what I took to be protestations of innocence. I didn't understand him; he used words found in no French Grammar, but it seemed Louie was familiar with the more idiomatic phrases. He listened with interest then said, "God in heaven, she's the *Dook's* chicken. *L'amie de Monsieur le Duc.*" He turned to me. "Tell him, miss."

While Louie could understand the patois and I could not, it was I who could speak French a little better, but still I felt some reluctance to say I was the Duke's chicken, and doubted that it would carry much weight in any case. Louie was good enough for me.

He turned back to the Frenchman. "He'll kill you!" he warned. "*Tuer — mort!*" Then he made a cutting gesture across his own throat that was quite unmistakable. "I'd better get the Dook," he said to me, but uncertainly.

"He is not at home. He's in London," I said. "Let me go back home — up the stairs." I indicated the bolted door.

He stood frowning. "That's how you got here?" he asked.

"Yes, I heard noises from the fireplace and came to investigate." I was rapidly recovering my powers of thought and speech with Louie's presence.

"I don't know that I can do that," he said. "I'd better get the Dook."

"He's not home I tell you."

"He's home."

I was sufficiently alert now to wonder how Louie should know this, but it would be a matter of some interest to the smugglers, perhaps, and I didn't quibble with the idea of getting him if he was home. "Very well. Get him. I'll wait at home."

Louie frowned again, still in uncertainty. I was beginning to realize that while he reacted quickly in a physical way, he was no deep problem-solver. "I can't let you go," he said simply.

"You can't leave me here with that animal!" I pointed to the Frenchman, who suddenly looked rather harmless, slouching in a corner.

"Yes, but I can't let you go, and the Dook might not come back here for hours."

"He will be coming *here* — *back here*?" I asked, while a thousand new conjectures arose. He had been here already, knew the place existed. He had somehow discovered where the smugglers were hiding the brandy. This was the direction of my first thoughts, but before long I was wandering off in a new direction. He had known all along! This was why he had wanted to get me out of Seaview; this was why he had been with Louie in the meadow; this was why he had objected to my excavation. *He was one of them.*

"Certainly he will have to come to tell us where . . ." He stopped, still frowning. "Damme, Miss Denver, what are we to do?" Louis asked, like a puzzled schoolboy. "I think I ought to fetch him."

"Send him," I said, indicating the Frenchman with a jerk of my head to the corner. There was no doubt in my mind which smuggler I would prefer to spend the interval with.

202

"He don't know the way, and besides the Dook would have my head if I sent that Frenchie to Belview for everyone to see. And he don't speak a word of English, either."

"Isn't there anyone else you could send?"

"No, the stuff is stored in the passageway, and they've all gone off home, the fellows."

The stuff — brandy. Confirmation they were smugglers, and the Duke of Clavering one of their number. With his insufferable airs and his claiming to think it a crime, he was not only a half-cousin to Lazy Louie but he was also his partner. The partner in command, I hadn't a doubt. And he refused to speak to his cousin when he met him on the street! Strange it did not occur to me that this was hardly a safe person to bring to my aid, but as he represented my means of getting home, I wanted him to come. I was really very eager to see how he behaved himself amongst his "Gentlemen" friends.

"We can't stay here," I pointed out. "They'll miss me at home. Call out a search party, and you'll have the whole countryside down here, seeing your smuggled brandy."

"No, dash it, we can't do that. I'll have to fetch him."

"Take me with you."

"In your nightgown?" he asked, scandalized. I had forgotten this detail, not that it would have stopped me from going. "I won't be gone a minute. You tell the Frenchie you're the Dook's girl, and he won't lay a hand on you."

"Don't you dare go and leave me!" I shouted, and it was necessary to shout, for he was already gone, back into the black hole and down the passage. I looked at the Frenchman, and he looked at me measuringly.

"*Ne touchez pas. Le Duc est mon ami. Très bon ami,*" I told him, trying to add heavy emphasis, in case the words were not quite accurate or comprehensible to him. I hadn't tried to speak French for years.

He sat down, lit a foul-smelling cigar, and sulked. I arose boldly and retrieved the candelabrum from the floor, relit the other tapers and began walking around the room to see what it was. It had a dirt floor and three stone walls. The third wall had once been muralled on plaster, I thought. Faint traces of outline were visible in the poor light. A painted series of arches, and the outline of a flowing gown in one of the arches. An unlikely decoration for a fort, which, of course, this was not. There were two straw mattresses on the floor, a table made of packing crates, and some food on the table. I looked over my shoulder at the Frenchman as I made my little tour, not at all sure he would remain harmless. And I was right. He stamped out his cigar half-smoked, and came toward me. My heart thumped with fright. I had no clock, had no idea how long Louie had been gone. Ten or fifteen minutes, I guessed — but how long would it take him to get to Belview and come back with the Duke?

My guard-prisoner was impressed enough with my claims on the Duke that he only lifted the light from my fingers and held it to the wall himself. He then took it to the barrels in the corner and set it on the floor, took up a tin cup and pulled the cork from the bunghole of one of them. A stream of dark liquid poured out sending its aroma across the room, and he drank it down as though it were water. He smacked his lips, wiped them with his sleeve, and regarded me with a bad smile.

The room had reeked of brandy when I first entered. There were half a dozen cups on the floor. They had all been drinking down here before, including the Duke of Clavering. The Frenchman might be half-drunk already, for all I knew. I turned away and walked to the furthest corner from him. I soon heard him having another helping of the smuggled brandy. It was stored in the passageway, but these two kegs must have been brought in for their own use, and good use they were making of them, too.

I was terrified he would get drunk and attack me. "*Ne buvez pas*," I commanded in a stern voice. He looked at me, smiled boldly, and took another drink. I issued no more commands, for I didn't wish to anger him. I just stood, glancing at him from time to time, and every time I looked he was examining me steadily. He didn't even move his eyes to drink. How long it was taking them! Why didn't they come?

At last it happened. He set down his cup and advanced toward me. There was no hesitation this time. He put both his arms around my waist and pulled me into his arms. Not without some resistance on my part, as you may imagine. I pushed at his chest, kicked his shins with my soft, harmless slippers. He was no taller than I was. Our eyes and lips were exactly level, yet he had, even in his drunken condition, three times my strength.

"*Le Duc vous tuera! Il est mon ami,*" I reminded him with panting gasps. He fixed one hand behind my head and pulled it rudely toward his brandy-soaked lips.

My French deserted me. "Don't! Don't touch me! I'm the Duke's friend. He'll . . ."

"Kill you!" Clavering said, in quite a polite tone, and suddenly my attacker was being lifted six inches off the floor and flung aside as though he were an empty coat.

In my struggle with the Frenchman I had not heard their approach, Clavering's and Louie's, but how glad I was to see them. Smugglers, bastards, criminals — whatever they were, they were welcome. I threw myself gratefully and shamelessly into Clavering's arms and heaved a sob of relief. He held me closely for a moment and said nothing, but I could hear his heart pound from his recent dash from Belview. His coat was wet and cool — it was still raining, then — and felt rough against my cheek. His hands moved up and down on my back comfortingly.

"You shouldn't have left her alone with that maniac," he said to Louie over my shoulder, then bent his head down to mine. "It's all right, Prissie. He wouldn't really have harmed you, you know. Come now, don't cry. I'll take you home."

Home, though it was only yards away, had such a reassuring sound to it! "Yes, take me home," I said, and pulled away from his arms. There was a little delay while Louie lit their own candles from mine, then

Clavering took up the candelabrum and followed me to the door, slid the bolt, and we walked up the narrow stairs into the parson's bench — such a foolish mode of entry to a room — climbed over its side and stood in the dimly lit saloon.

"Close the lid," I said, for I didn't want even that reminder of where I had been, and what I had been through.

"Sit down. I'll get you some wine," he said. I sank on to a sofa and sat benumbed, not yet recovered enough to be angry or outraged or anything but grateful that I was home safe.

He handed me a glass and sat down beside me. Apparently under the misapprehension that I still required comfort, he put an arm around my shoulders. "He didn't do any worse than try to kiss you?" he asked.

"No, but he would have," I replied, removing his arm.

"Louie's a fool. Well-meaning, but to leave you alone . . . Drink your wine. It will calm you."

"I don't want to be calm. I want an explanation."

"All in good time," he answered calmly. "Isn't it strange to be here alone in the middle of the night? Very intimate, don't you think?"

"Clavering . . ."

"Don't you think you should call your friend Burne," he suggested, turning to smile lazily at me.

"You're not my friend."

"Except when you are in trouble. I heard you use me to threaten André."

"If it weren't for you I wouldn't have been in trouble! How *dare* you use my house for smuggling?"

"Not your house, Prissie. *My* land that is temporarily leased to you. Unfortunately it abuts against the wall of your house, but really, you know, I offered a dozen times to buy it from you and save you this unpleasant episode. I had the sinking feeling that sooner or later you'd get into the parson's bench. The door at the bottom of the stairs was always kept bolted, by the way. I guess André must have heard you trying to break it down, and decided to let you in?"

"How could you expect me *not* to discover it, when you were laughing and carousing down there to wake the dead?"

"I thought you'd be safely asleep in your bed by that time. I tried to keep the noise down to a roar, but after a successful trip the boys always have a round. What were you doing up and all alone at such an hour?"

"It's my house! I don't have to explain to you why I am up."

"You don't have to explain why you decided to go investigating all alone in your chemise, either, but it does seem unlike the practical Miss Denver. Quite like the impractical one who tries to ride a nag she can't handle, though, now I come to think of it."

"Don't try to shift the blame for this night's work on to *me*. You have a great deal of explaining to do."

"I have, and I shall do it tomorrow. You're too upset now. In your excitement the impropriety of our situation has slipped your mind. I have no objection in the least to your entertaining me in such charming *deshabillé*, but Slack might misunderstand."

"I am not entertaining you."

"You noticed that, too, did you? I am happy to see we agree on what constitutes entertainment. I think that as we have allowed all the other proprieties to go by the boards, we might as well go all the way and dabble in a little entertainment. Why should André be the only one to enjoy the night's work? And you *did* tell him you are my friend, you know. I believe I even heard the word *tuera* being mentioned. Now I don't go *killing* every fellow who makes advances to a lady unless she is *my* lady."

"Don't you dare lay a hand on me!" I said in a low voice, for we had been speaking low to avoid detection by any light sleeper.

"I never can resist a dare," he answered promptly, and laid not one hand but two on my shoulders, pulling me roughly into his arms. He soon placed his lips as well on mine and was kissing me soundly. Had I not already suffered so many unusual adventures that night, I might have been more outraged, but somehow it seemed a suitable climax to the evening. Even it seemed to soothe my jangled nerves. I did not bother to fight him off and give him the idea it mattered; it would have pleased him too well. I let him embrace me and enjoyed it, but did not actively participate. It was my first kiss. Edward Hemmings (my first beau, if my reader has forgotten) talked a good deal about love but was not a great man for action. I underwent the thing

209

as though it were an experiment, trying to analyse the sensation of being held and mauled a little by a man.

After a while he lifted his head. "You can do better than that, Priss," he said teasingly. "Another first, I trust?"

"Yes, unless you include your French smuggler friend."

"That explains it. Practice makes perfect. Don't be afraid."

"I don't need any lessons."

"Yes, you do. It is like riding, and can be taught. Relax and enjoy it." He kissed me again, more strenuously, but I don't think he followed his own advice. He was not the least relaxed, but became sufficiently ardent that I was obliged to struggle free.

"Oh, you're coming on rapidly," he said with approval. "A natural. You'll be giving me lessons before the week's out." He put his hand on the back of my head, just like the Frenchman, but I pulled it away, for I was a little frightened of my own feelings. I had not thought the whole body reacted so violently to a kiss.

"That's enough of that," I said primly.

"Not near enough. I've been wishing I'd done this since I took my leave of you; if you'd been in your usual sparring trim I would have. You're a very attractive woman, Prissie, hard as you try to conceal it with your modest dress. And you were right; Prissie is the wrong name, thank God. I was half afraid you'd be a cold one."

I expect I was still suffering a little from my ordeal in the cellar, or I would have stopped him sooner, but when he tried to resume kissing me I objected strongly. "See here, Clavering . . ."

"You have the most sensuous lips I've ever kissed," he said, leaning toward me with his hands out.

This was not to be trusted, nor endured. "Burne!"

"I am aflame, my love. I have been for ages. You can even shout a 'Wed' at me and I won't take it amiss. Someone is singing it in my ears already."

"That would be your conscience, if you have one! I think you had better go now," I said, pulling my dressing-gown tightly about me. Not to say that it was open; it wasn't, but the belt was working loose.

"I might as well, if you mean to lock up all the sweets." I glared at him, shocked at such a bold speech. "All right, Priss, I'm going." He arose.

"I hope there is some way you can keep that menacing Frenchman out of my house."

"I trust Louie has taken care of him by now, and if he hasn't, you may be sure I will. What would you like me to do with him? Put him on the rack — pull out his fingernails — cut out his tongue. Remember the temptation the poor fellow was subjected to. And he is French, you know." He walked to the parson's bench and lifted the lid.

"Well, *au revoir*. Time to crawl into the bench. Ah, listen, my Prissie, you won't do anything foolish like run to Officer Smith with this story, will you? I shall be back early in the morning to explain everything."

I don't remember what I said. I recall he stood on the first rung of the stairway leading below, and very nearly tumbled over, cracking his shins when he reached out toward me and I stepped back suddenly. I also remember he uttered some ungentlemanly oaths, but apologized.

"Shall I tell Slack?" I asked. I must have been still in shock to ask such a question, to ask permission to do it, I mean.

"Suit yourself," he answered curtly. "It is clear you have no intention of further humouring me. Good night, Miss Priss."

CHAPTER
FOURTEEN

The minute Clavering was gone, I put down the bench lid and placed on top of it the heaviest things I could find in the room. Some of his own tomes on Roman ruins, some blocks of wood, a large fern in a nice heavy pot, and other smaller oddments. Then I went to bed. Not that I had any thoughts of sleeping after such a night. I lay awake for hours, thinking. Firstly, I wondered how I had been deranged enough in my mind to have let him away without getting a full explanation of his part in this criminal smuggling business. It must have been shock, pure and simple. My mind was not functioning properly after such an ordeal, and his love-making hadn't helped clear it, either. In fact, he had very likely kissed me to make me forget it, and as it was a new experience for me, it had succeeded; but the morning was coming, and I would have my revenge. He would explain his web of lies over the past weeks. His pretending not to know about the Roman ruins next door, his close association with Louie and the smuggling. How did he come to be embroiled in these low pursuits? Was it a love of excitement and danger? If so, why not involve himself in the war with Napoleon? Plenty of chance there for any reckless, danger-loving man to combine duty and pleasure.

With so much to consider, sleep was impossible. I saw the sun rise through my window, a beautiful golden-rose glow that promised another fine day. As it crept above the treetops, I began to consider rising, then my eyes closed at last and I slept — till noon. I was furious when I awoke and glanced at the clock. Why had no one awakened me? Before many moments I was up, dressed, and hurtling down the stairs. I ran first to the saloon, to see that someone had moved the obstacles from the lid of the parson's bench. The room was empty. I ran next to the morning parlour, to be confronted with the spectacle of Miss Slack hovering over Clavering's shoulder, pouring him a cup of coffee and smiling gaily.

"Well, young lady," she said. "I think you might have included *me* in your little adventure last night."

"You told her?" I asked Burne.

"You know these women. They always worm all your secrets out of you."

"Then she has done a good deal better than I have, for it seems to me I managed to let you off without an explanation, and I am eager to hear it now."

"I am eager to give it. Do sit down and have a cup of coffee, Priss." *My* home and *my* coffee! Kind of him to allow me to enjoy them.

"This is the last cup. I'll pour it and get some more," Slack said, but she was only being discreet again, and leaving us alone.

"I must say, you don't look any the worse after last night's frolic," he said, with his eyes lingering on my face.

"Never mind thinking to trick me out of an explanation with that old stunt. I mean to hear why you have taken to smuggling with your cousin, Louie Fitzhugh."

"Officer Smith, I understand, is your informant? Well, it's true enough. Louie is one of my family connections."

"How nice for you!" I said, settling back with my coffee.

"Convenient, certainly. He is the best seaman in Pevensey. Louie could land a ship in the middle of a howling storm without wetting the decks. But, of course, he's part Clavering, and that must explain his skill."

"As well as that little streak of larceny that seems to run in the Clavering blood."

"Quite. We have some fine gold plate and jewelled crosses at home that one of our ancestors helped himself to in Peru when he was sailing with Sir Francis Drake. We have been at it for centuries."

"Shall we dispense with ancient history and get right down to the present pirate in the family?"

"Smuggler. There is a shade of difference. Louis is a smuggler only. Well, throw in bribing officials, to revert to history."

"But not the only smuggler, nor only briber of officials, either."

"It gets dull, you know, sitting in the House in London, listening to long-winded speeches, then coming home and talking to tenant farmers and bailiffs. Everyone needs a little excitement in his life."

"Not everyone chooses to indulge his whim by turning smuggler, and even those who *do* do not in the general way set themselves up as pillars of rectitude, looking down on the smuggling community. And I think you must surely be the only aristocratic smuggler in all of England."

"No, no. I can tell you for a fact my cousin, Lord Tremaine, is also active. He operates from Dover."

"Well, upon my word! And you said not a month ago you were going to replace Officer Smith because he is not wide-awake enough!"

"But I didn't do it, you notice. His somnolent manner of proceeding suits me very well."

"Clavering, do you mean to sit there and tell me unashamedly that you are a *smuggler*?" I demanded in astonishment, for I was sure he'd try to put some good face on it.

"I am a little ashamed," he confessed. "But there's no real harm in it. It keeps Louie and the boys out of worse mischief."

"If you were ever found out, you would be *disgraced*."

"It would be embarrassing, and that is why I am come to ask if you could find it in your heart to overlook the events of last night."

"You're asking me to conspire in crime?"

"Not actually take an active part. 'Watch the wall, my darling.' It is an old . . ."

"Yes, I know all about it. George told me. Good God! Is George in on this, too?"

"He doesn't work with my group," Clavering answered blandly.

"Then you admit you are in charge. You called it your group."

"You didn't expect me to take commands from Louie FitzHugh? I organize the runs, but we use Lou's ship, the *Nancy-Jane*, and he is the better sailor, so he is the captain of the ship. Nominally he is in command at sea, I suppose. A difference has not arisen on the high seas to put it to the test."

"You mean you actually go to France with them?" The more he talked, the less could I credit that he was telling the truth.

"That's the best part. The rest of it is *work*."

"And that's where you've been these past days, when you let it out that you were in London at Parliament?"

"Yes, we got back last evening, in the teeth of a booming gale, but Cousin Louie is up to anything. You spoke of my deception in making clear my displeasure with the smugglers, but that keeps Smith pretty well away from my stretch of coast, you know. I have my own patrol out, so he doesn't bother with it. He feels they wouldn't dare land here, and my warnings of mantraps keep the lands free of trespassers who are likely to disturb us in transit from sea to chapel, so we have pretty clear running. I don't think there is much risk of being discovered. Really, I think I have devised an admirable arrangement."

"I doubt Leo Milkin, the cripple at the inn, would agree with you. To gain freedom of detection in *criminal* proceedings at the cost of crippling probably dozens of men . . ."

"There is not a mantrap of any kind on any of my land."

"But you've posted your signs, and killed all your foxes!"

"Oh, killing my poor foxes, that was the hardest part of the whole thing. How I hated to part with them. But as to the signs, it is not illegal to post without actually laying the traps. I looked into it. It is illegal to trap without posting, but not to post without trapping."

"How did the man at the inn come to be crippled then, eel?"

"He fell into an excavation at the ruined chapel one night he was drunk, and broke or sprained his ankle. As I had posted my signs the day before, it was generally assumed he was my first victim, and as it proved so efficacious in keeping others away, I did nothing to allay the rumour. In fact, he was paid handsomely to drag his limb around town and tell everyone he met what had happened to him, as a warning."

"You actually *paid* the man to blacken your character?"

"No, just to lie a little."

"Yes, you're fond of that. The lies you've been telling me. You knew all the time why my grate was shaking, with your men rolling their brandy around and banging against the walls, and you let me go on worrying."

"It was accidental at first. I was away, first in London and later in France when you came here, and by the time I got back you had already bought up Seaview. If only I had known your aunt wished to sell, what a lot of bother we would both have been saved. I really am eager to restore the bite to the tip of my piece of pie. I would have bought it gladly, even if it had been standing empty. But no, you were in and complaining of the noisy chimney before I knew what was happening. It was accidental the first time, but when you spoke of ghosts and proved impervious to all my lies and bribery, we decided to see if we couldn't scare you out. I went down one night and Louie the next morning and gave the wall a couple of good boots. But you reciprocated by calling in Pickering to hint you toward the parson's bench, and when you began speaking of excavating . . ."

"And you knew all along that there was no fort underneath Seaview."

"I regretted I had chosen a *fort* when I remembered the remains of one at Pevensey, just three miles away. Once Slack took up an interest in the hobby I was in constant dread she would tumble to it."

"I was the one who tumbled to it. I knew it couldn't be another fort. What is it, by the way?"

"The remains of a villa. The wall that forms one foundation wall of your cellar is part of a drawing-room. Rather a nice mural on one wall, but badly deteriorated. It was a large affair, the villa, covering the better part of an acre. Must have been a pretty wealthy gent. I believe my little ruined chapel is built on the remains of some private temple, for it is too small to have been for public use. My great-grandfather is the one who made the discoveries, and first became interested in all this digging business. When he built Seaview, he had dug out most of the land between the chapel and there, and put in the underground tunnel at that time. It runs from the chapel to the foundation of your cellar, and up into your parson's bench, of course. I can't think why he did it, for there was an unusual period of peace prevailing at the time, under Robert Walpole. But we had just made peace with France after the Spanish Succession Wars, and it may have been thought the peace would not long be with us. Nor was it, in historical time lengths. Or it might have been done to give easy but private access to the remains of the villa without laying them open to the elements. In any case, he had the tunnel built, and it is an excellent place to hide the goods."

"I don't see why you have to bring it all the way into the room that joins my house."

"We don't. It is left about ten feet inside the mouth of the tunnel, but that room is the only one in good repair, with all the walls standing. The rest of them are crumbling badly. In fact, they are shored up, and the tunnel leads to only that one room. I have the plans of the villa at home, but only that one room is actually open, and it is an excellent place for the men to hide out, for they can't hang about in Pevensey, you know,

220

and I certainly don't want a gang of Frenchies at Belview causing talk."

"How does it come you use Frenchmen? I should think if you are going to break the law and smuggle, you might at least let the profits go to Englishmen."

A look of guilty surprise flew across his face, and I suddenly realized he was lying still. "Clavering, you eel! You haven't told me a word of truth. What are you up to?"

"Why would I tell you lies of a nature so unflattering to myself? Of course it is true. I use mostly Englishmen, but a few Frenchies help us."

"I know perfectly well you are lying. I don't know what you're really doing, but I know it's not this, or this is not all of it, at least."

"Well, what do you think I'm doing? Smuggling arms to France for Boney to use against us? Sending money across the Channel illegally to finance him and his campaigns? Dammit, Prissie, I'm an *Englishman*! You've seen some of the brandy yourself. You know it's there," he said angrily.

"If I thought for one minute you were helping Napoleon Bonaparte I'd report you so fast your head would spin."

"I would have a very poor opinion of you if you didn't."

"You *promise* me you're not?"

"How can you doubt it?" he demanded, furious. "That damned upstart has spilled the blood of thousands of Englishmen, my own cousins and friends slaughtered, to say nothing of the country virtually bankrupted. This war has cost us close to a *billion* pounds and will exceed that before it's over. This, while millions of our people go poor and hungry. Any man who would aid him should be drawn and quartered. It is the duty of each of us to do what he can . . ." He pulled himself up to a stop. "Well, I may be a smuggler, but you may be sure I am not helping Napoleon Bonaparte in any way."

"So that's it!" I said, and put down my coffee cup. I smiled at him. "You might have told me, Burne."

"I have told you."

"You haven't told me what you are really doing, but I am not a complete ninnyhammer, I hope."

"Priss, what do you . . ."

"I won't ask embarrassing questions. I know you spies have to work in secrecy."

"What foolish notion have you taken into your head now?"

"I have taken the notion, not completely foolish, I think, for I had it of a gentleman whose intelligence I trust, that you are sneaking into France as a smuggler to find out exactly what is going on there. Looking to see if there is a surprise attack being planned, or some such thing."

"What, an attack with Boney's hands full fighting the Prussians? What are you talking about?"

"I don't know, but I expect you do. There is news to be picked up on the coast of France, I imagine."

"The coast? Lord, no, you have to go further inland than that," he answered, abandoning his idea of keeping me in ignorance.

222

"Oh, Burne, I hope you are careful."

"I am very careful, since I have so much to come home to. Louie tells me I'm turning chicken-livered only because I refused to help him kidnap a French colonel we saw straggling along the streets of Amiens. But as we would have had to drag him sixty or seventy miles to our ship, I felt it better to soak his insides with brandy and strain out information from him there."

"Is that the sort of thing you do?"

"We indulge in various pastimes. Loiter around the less genteel cafés and inns, and visit some known connections — paid informers. Not every Frenchman backs Napoleon."

"Will there be an attack, do you think?"

"He could hardly muster enough men to launch a smuggling boat at this time. There are no troops built up on the coast to speak of. With the Prussians in the north and the Iron Duke coming up at him from the south, he hasn't time to think of it. Next time I'll try to make it all the way to Paris and . . ."

"Next time! You're not going again?"

"Just have my leash ready for me, Prissie. It won't be much longer. I have to do it, you know."

"Don't worry, I'm not planning to bridle you."

"Leash, love. I said leash. I trust you walk a dog with more skill than you ride a horse, or my life isn't worth a Birmingham farthing."

"I'm sure I don't follow the tenor of these assorted animal references. I recall your antipathy to marriage, and I assure you I don't want a pet duke in the kennels, or the stables, either."

"I had some hopes I would be permitted right into the saloon if I behaved myself. I don't have fleas, and neither scratch nor bite, and after all, it is my house."

"Oh, it is Belview we are discussing. As you make yourself so free of Willow Hall, I thought it was here you were talking about. You must be lonely, of course, at home, with all those empty bedrooms — *rooms* — but . . ."

"You were right the first time. It is the bedrooms I find especially lonesome. As to my former views on marriage . . ."

"Not two weeks ago you were talking it down, saying you would rather jump from a housetop."

"The battle was already lost. It was the death rattle of a trapped man. After seeing you exactly four times — being subjected to abuse at every encounter, too — and forcing myself to stay away for a week when I saw what peril I was running into, I gave it up. With your aunt pushing George at your head, I realized I'd have to marry you myself. You have no resistance to a bad bargain, and I was afraid you'd have him. I was quite disgusted with myself to see my carefully nurtured philosophy of misogamy being torn to shreds."

"You forget both Miss Slack and I share that philosophy with you."

"That was a low trick! Pretending to agree with me, so that I was forced to play the devil's advocate."

"You're well qualified for the job."

"It is one that requires a certain objectivity and intelligence that I am rather well qualified to supply, I suppose."

"Those weren't the qualifications I had in mind. And I know perfectly well you only want to get hold of Seaview, so don't bother trying to gull me."

"Oh, no, Priss. I think you know perfectly well it's you I want to take hold of, and if you would drink up that coffee, I think I might do it before I have to leave."

"You keep your great paws to yourself! Just because I let you . . . because you took advantage . . ." I came to a stuttering stop, not quite liking to say he had forced me.

He looked at his well-shaped hands and glanced up questioningly. "*Paws*, eh? Was I that rough with you? My hands have always been considered my one attractive feature. You hit me in a tender spot."

"We scarcely know each other at all, and it is absurd to speak of marriage, if that is what we are speaking of."

"Is that why you quibble? Certainly I mean to do the thing up right and legally — for the sake of the children, you know. There are enough Louies floating around the parish without our adding another generation of them."

"As neither law-breaking nor illegitimacy is looked down on by you, I was not sure you meant to avail yourself of a preacher."

He looked steadily at me and smiled in good humour, refusing to take umbrage at any of my jibes. "Come, put down that cup before Slack gets back. Let us have a look at the parson's bench and see what should be done with it. We must nail the lid down, at least."

Not so slow as he took me for, I had a pretty sharp idea why he wished to draw me into the private saloon, and doubted the bench had anything to do with it. He meant to make a proper offer, and I looked forward with the greatest pleasure to turning him down. How surprised he would be! He kept on talking while we walked into the hall, where Wilkins was rearranging the umbrellas in their container, as he did every time I passed by, to give the impression of being busy. "It is true we have not known each other long, but I generally come to a swift assessment of my friends, and I think you are not different in that respect."

"I have had *your* measure for some time, in any case."

We went into the saloon, and he closed the door behind him. Without a single glance at the parson's bench, we sat on the sofa, the same we had occupied the night before.

He continued, "I know you are stubborn, foolish, headstrong, and a termagant. You must know by now that this unhandsome gypsy exterior of mine hides the character of a criminal, complete with a strong tendency to lie, manipulate people, dominate, and take unfair advantage. My family associations are nearly as bad as your own. I give you the slight edge in that respect, since you have both Lady Inglewood and George, whereas I have only Louie living close enough to annoy us. Now where, outside of heaven, would you find a better-suited pair?"

"At least you're not sensible!" I said, trying to register disapproval, but not quite succeeding.

"No, no, you will find very little in the way of common sense, elegance of mind, or such detriments to counterbalance my manifold advantages. Well, what do you say, Priss? Do you think you can handle me?" He worded his offer in terms impossible to reject, and his sly smile told me he knew it, manipulator.

"I could handle you or a dozen like you!"

"That's what I thought, but I hope you will limit yourself to one," he replied and snatched me into his arms in his characteristically common fashion, as if I were a servant wench. I had enough trouble controlling one aggressive animal bent on mischief that I fear I rather overstated my abilities in that respect. Licentiousness was clearly to be numbered amongst his major accomplishments. Not content to seal the engagement with the customary kiss, he went on to point out he would have to leave soon for London to report his findings, and therefore had three days' lovemaking coming to him, all of which he wished to make up in five minutes concentrated assault. I am afraid I was obliged to bolt to the fireplace and pick up a poker in my own defence, not that I would really have cleaved his head open, but it served to control him.

"Now that I am your lord and master — practically," he told me, regarding the poker a little fearfully, "I have a few commands to present to you. One, you not send a groom to my stables to retrieve Juliette and attempt to ride her during my absence. I want you in one unmutilated piece when I get back. I'll find something you can handle at Tatt's while I'm in the city. Two, you will stay out of the parson's bench. Three, you will stay out of the meadow. Four, you will have your wedding gown made up while I'm gone. I smuggled you a lovely piece of white silk and will bring it before I leave. And, love, don't feel obliged to have it made up into a grandmama's gown, like your others. I think I felt a waist on you last night, and would like to see it. If you could bring yourself to reveal a shoulder blade or wrist, I wouldn't mind, either."

"Thank you very much!"

He tossed up his hands and continued with his "commands," every one of which I would most certainly disobey. "Five, you will consult with Slack or your aunt or whomever you think can advise you on the proper method of throwing on a wedding with the utmost dispatch, without too much aroma of unseemly necessity to it."

"Burne — it takes weeks! There are banns and invitations and . . ."

"Nonsense! What do a pair of misogamists like us want with a formal do? Such carryings-on are to be executed with as much privacy as the disgraceful thing deserves. We don't want to be giving the villagers a bad example. I'll spirit back a licence, and we'll wed next week — *early* next week — right here in this room. I'll warn Louie to keep the boys away from the grate for the occasion." He stopped and looked at me closely.

"Or do you harbour under that stony exterior some romantic notions of orange blossoms and white lace?"

"Heavens, no! I'm in mourning, really, for my step-father, who isn't dead a year yet, but no one here knows it."

"Good." He stood up and straightened his tie, lifting his chin, and stretching his neck in that peculiar way men have and that seems to me to serve no purpose whatever. "Would you mind putting down the poker?" he asked, with a look in his eye I had already come to mistrust sadly.

As there was the sound of voices outside the door — Slack speaking to Wilkins — I put it down and we walked to the parson's bench as though we had been there the whole time. Slack entered carrying a fresh cup of coffee for me and with an inquisitive look on her face.

"Slack," Clavering said, "I am about to commit marriage with your girl, and I suppose I must explain a few things." He went on to tell her as much as I knew myself.

"I suspected something of the sort," she said calmly. "I knew, of course, it was nonsense that you were just smuggling. But is it necessary for you to work with the Frenchies, Burne? Do you trust them?"

"About as far as from here to that footstool. They've no idea what we're up to outside of smuggling, but it makes that end of it go more smoothly, and the Gentlemen have to make a living. I keep my Frenchies locked up in the villa, so there's no chance of their discovering anything while they're here. They smuggle back sugar and spices and the odd thing that is in short supply in France."

"I see. Well, it seems we have not given much talk to this wedding of yours. I want to express my congratulations to you both, and I hope you will be very happy. Have you thought where you will go for a wedding journey?"

"Burne is going to Paris with Louie for his wedding journey, and I am staying here with you," I told her.

"A little later we'll all go somewhere together," Clavering promised.

"All?" Slack asked with a laugh. "I hope I am not such a gugdeon that I plan to trail after you on your wedding journey."

"Ah, but it is Aquae Sulis we have in mind, Slack," he tempted.

Her eyes sparkled with desire, but she laughed. "I will return to Wilton. There will be good digging there. Archaeological digging, I mean."

"My dear, if you are not part of the dowry, I must beg off," he told her. "Who will help me discover the glories of our buried villa after the war is over? There is our museum — so much to be done there. I really *do* plan to set one up, you know, and you can imagine what little help this addlepated bride of mine will be. She wouldn't know a mosaic from a mural. Besides, I plan to keep her chained to her household duties — and the nursery. Tell her, Prissie."

"Slack, you can't abandon me to this monster! If I have to choose between the two of you, I choose *you!*"

"Really, Slack, you two were engaged first. Prissie gave you the diamond on your birthday. I see the whole thing crumbling before my eyes. *I* am to be left in the lurch," he declared. "I'll sue you both for breach of promise."

Slack laughed merrily, for of course she never had the least thought of deserting us but only felt it polite to make the gesture. "I begin to think the pair of you need a nanny," she said.

"We do!" Burne assured her. "And look how convenient my library will be for you. I'll get my books back. We will have the cosiest *menage à trois* outside of Devonshire House."

"I'll think about it," Slack condescended, but there was not a vestige of doubt in any of our minds. The thing was settled.

"Well, darlings, I'm off," Burne said. "I'll be back in three days and expect my brides to be ready for me. I'll see my chaplain before I go. If you want to start removing your things to Belview while I'm gone, just send a note over. I'll speak to my people to help you. Now, have we forgotten anything? You'll see to the nailing down of the bench, Slack? And if you hear any merriment below, remember how the smuggling community is to be dealt with. Sit on the bench, my darlings!"

He blew us a kiss and left.

CHAPTER
FIFTEEN

31 October, 1813

Napoleon was defeated at Leipzig on 19 October and has retired into Paris. With the armies of the present coalition hounding him, it is unnecessary for Burne to continue his little trips. Indeed he *says* even Cousin Louie no longer goes, but I notice Officer Smith continues to keep a close eye on *Nancy-Jane*, and our own patrols continue to roam the coast, flashing a signal from the best spot for landing. Nor do I perceive any shortage of brandy in Burne's decanter, which he uses only for medicinal purposes, of course! I am forced to the conclusion that despite his hardy appearance he has some chronic ailment, for the level goes down and up regularly. Slack is no help in controlling his intake. She has succumbed completely to his blandishments and his library (and dried cherries), but I do not mean to imply he has become a drunkard. That refinement is lacking.

He speaks of setting up his museum, and speaks, too, of taking us through the tunnel to view the ruins, but has not done either. One afternoon while he was at the village on business, Slack and I went to Seaview and pried up the lid of the parson's bench, but the door at the bottom of the stairs was bolted, so we had to go to the meadow and eventually found the entrance from the ruined chapel. It was well concealed behind bushes and piles of stone, but we discovered it and entered it with torches and examined the one room. There was little enough to see I thought, but Slack is itching to return and have another try at discovering the artist who executed the mural. He was no Michelangelo, I'll say that. There was no mosaic floor under the ruined chapel at all. That was just one more lie. Seaview stands empty awaiting a nice deaf couple who will not be bothered by rattling grates. It is not to be used for the museum, but a building is to be erected in Pevensey. My husband tells me that as it is my "nagging" that caused this decision, I will be expected to dip heavily into Mr Higgins's money to help defray the cost. I knew how it would be.

Our journey to Bath draws close. We have already had one short one to Londinium, just the two of us. If the trip to Bath is anything like it, it will be horrid. You will have noticed I said, "Londinium." No, I have not fallen into the revolting habit of using the names of yore. We didn't see a thing of London. We tramped through basements of shops and even private dwellings to see walls and pavements of Londinium, and also drove to out-of-the-way spots high up on hills to admire the old city walls. It was Londinium we visited, and I am instituting a campaign to return in the spring to attend some concerts and plays and balls. A reference to Lady Inglewood and George I find useful in this scheme. I have only to hint she would be happy to accompany her "dear niece, the Duchess" as she calls me now, if my husband is too engaged, and Burne will suddenly find that he can manage "a week or two" for the enterprise. We will stay a month, however.

For our honeymoon to Bath, Slack is fashioning herself a bathing robe and expresses the intention of placing her feet where those thousands of Roman feet have trod at the diving stone. I trust she won't slip and fall in, for she can't swim a stroke. She is almost totally out of black these days. Her beau prefers his ladies in colours. She tells me I needn't tease her, for I am practically out of my gowns altogether. This is an ill-natured reference to the fact that I have two evening gowns that show my shoulders and arms, but I am not totally depraved. I usually wear my white shawl, even when Burne stokes up the fire so that I nearly melt. He claims he still couldn't swear I have a waist.

Our wedding was carried out with the utmost secrecy, as though it were a crime. Only Lady Inglewood and George were there on my side, both with faces as long as though it were a funeral they were attending. The other smuggler in my husband's family, Lord Tremaine, and his wife came from Dover, but Louie was too lazy to come. He calls on us occasionally, and I like him excessively. In fact, he has become my beau, as Clavering is Slack's. I tell Burne he must not be jealous since I owe both my life and my virtue to Louie's quick thinking.

Under Louie's rough exterior there lurks the soul of a pet kitten. He is gentle and bashful. I mean to find him a bride and reform him. My own groom is sufficiently docile that I am ready to bear-lead his cousin, as well. I received from London a mount slightly less incorrigible than Juliette, by no means tame. Lady Ing got Juliette back from Clavering by some unknown means, by which I mean an unknown price. She is looking very smug, and I *think* she got it without any expense at all. She gave us what purports to be her late husband's Roman collection for a wedding gift — two books and a box of bent coins and "artifacts." We have been nearly totally relieved of George's visits. He is dangling after some girl in the village who seems much inclined to encourage him. The girl is not so blue blooded as Lady Ing could like, but the necessary tinge of gold is strong, and my aunt seems resigned to the match.

I have come to the end of my story, or the end of writing it, in any case. I do not consider life over, nor its excitement likely to diminish. We have as yet contrived no incipient increase in the population, but it is early days yet for that. I am very busy being mistress of a large home, head of half a dozen local charities, matchmaker, and wife. It has been suggested to me by Clavering that I show a quite amazing disregard for my priorities. Wife should come first, or in any case not last. I soothe him by saying I leave the best for the last, but he is not convinced and wonders if we are not blood relations in some fashion, since I seem to be something of an eel myself. There — down to seven *I*'s in my last paragraph, and I hope less of an egotist than when I (nine) began.